VANISHING
A PURPOSE DRIVEN JIHAD

OC CUSTER, JR.

Wasteland Press

www.wastelandpress.net
Shelbyville, KY USA

Vanishing: A Purpose Driven Jihad
by OC Custer, Jr.

First Printing – July 2015
ISBN: 978-1-68111-044-8

Printed in the U.S.A.

0   1   2   3

For the brilliant, yet somehow blinded American women – that they may awaken and rise up versus the metastasizing horror of sharia

American Continuum

On a single lane road which was little more than a footpath, Jake Harwell rounded a bend and found himself obstructed by a small herd of bison. There were perhaps twenty-five of the great shaggy beasts in front of his truck and, instead of blowing the horn or continuing on to ease his way through, he simply stopped and turned off the engine. He rolled down the window, then was very still; watching, listening. And, after only a couple of minutes, the animals seemed to forget about him, returning to their various activities.

Several grazed on the lush green grass alongside; one laid down on her back, "dust bathing"; while directly in front and on the road, a mother allowed her light colored young to suckle. Then finally, the largest bull – the leader – who it seemed had not forgotten, walked slowly, deliberately up to the window and peered down and in, his eyes burning fierce in the great dark head.

It seemed like a long time that he stood there, and Jake didn't move, didn't breathe – hoping the giant wouldn't take a sudden dislike and begin ramming and butting the pick-up's near side. More than one such incident had occurred, he knew, and understood that the bull was warning him.

Nothing happened though. With a snort, the bull finally moved away – which Jake took as a sign of at least tacit acceptance. And everything else continued on, and had continued – another cow took a dust bath; another mother suckled her young; and others grazed alongside.

So that then, he began to get an uncanny feeling of forever timelessness – a deliberateness which registered dimly at first, as he was groping for its meaning. In fact too, after he and the little herd had been there together for some 30 or 40 minutes, he was realizing a kind of mystical connection to the whole continuum – to their bison ancestors who had grazed, bathed and suckled in the same manner in the same spot, and doubtless been hunted there too by generations of Native Americans who were so dependent upon them.

Presently, he got out of the truck and relieved himself, their lack of response a further sign of acceptance. He stood with them for several minutes then, silent and listening to their various grunts and snortings. Then back inside, considered again the dependent relationship the Indians had had with them, and the terrible void left when white men had conducted their planned ethnic cleansing slaughter. It had been, he now understood, not just a loss of resource for the Indians, but a loss of family.

In those days, Jake Harwell shot video for TV specials all over the West, but mostly in Montana, Wyoming and the Dakotas. Becoming steeped in American history and ever further removed from the norms of traffic, shopping malls and nonsense.

CHAPTER ONE

It was the pastor's wife, Amy, who began raising red flags regarding the country's direction, or misdirection. But typically, Pastor Benjamin Brown ignored her. Or rather, placated her, secure in the confidence that his pursuit of ministry had raised him up, not only above Amy, but above virtually all of the laity. It was almost in fact an elevated sense of infallibility, perhaps akin to the papal claims in Rome.

Nevertheless, wife Amy was adamant. And he had never known her to be so resistant to his soothing conciliation.

"Now the Lord wouldn't have us to bicker, Amy," he said in his most syrupy tone. But, she just wasn't buying it. He was paunchy, dressed typically in a white short sleeve shirt and pleated tan pants; apple cheeked with mustache, lank brown hair and spectacles. He was eight years older than she, but it might as well have been twenty, given his air of superiority. They'd met at a conference sponsored by the Bible college she'd attended and their pairing up was one of those male-female mysteries which only God Himself might understand.

"Oh bullshit," she said, truly shocking him, as he'd never heard her utter such language.

"Don't you read the newspapers at all? I know you watch the TV news sometimes. Can't you see what's happening? Your pie in the sky prosperity message just marries up with the religion of materialism – which has left an absolute spiritual vacuum. People are worshipping and yearning after the almighty dollar. Not Jesus Christ!"

"Well, I can't agree, Amy," he said, nevertheless captivated as always by the flashing intelligence in her extraordinary gray eyes. She was tall, blond and slender; genuinely gentle albeit impertinent. And he was more than eager to forgive any transgression. "The Lord does want us all to prosper, and in that way our people can be an ever brighter beacon to the world."

He put his arms around her and she sobbed into his chest. "It's all right, love," he said, "you know I forgive you" – mistaking her sorrow as a plea for absolution when in fact she was grieving for what she perceived somewhere in her spirit as a vanishing way of life.

Somehow, there was always this disconnect. She warned him about the Muslims, too. "I always have this feeling that they hate us," she said, "and that they don't just want to worship peacefully, as everybody keeps saying."

"Well," he said with great reasonableness, "of course they want us all to be Muslims. But then, don't we want them to become Christians?"

"Yes, but we don't believe we should kill them if they don't convert!"

"Oh, I certainly don't believe the majority of Muslims believe that!"

"Oh really," her retort was irreverent, sassy, "what's happened to Christians in those countries where *sharia* law has been imposed? Or is in the process of being imposed? I wonder if the martyrs there are chanting incantations thankful for moderation as their heads are being chopped off!"

Intuitively, she recognized that something was afoot when two Mid-Eastern types – a man and his presumed wife – showed up at Sunday service. And they didn't just *show up*, but positioned themselves down near the front of the congregation. Short people – he in charcoal business suit, white shirt and no tie and she in the sort of modified *berka* that the women wear in the States, and with a checked blue handkerchief replacing the more traditional hooded bonnet.

Of course, Amy's husband, the right Reverend Benjamin Brown couldn't wait to get down from the platform after the service to welcome them – with all sorts of grandiose evangelizing bells no doubt clanging in his brain. There had been a noticeable influx to the neighborhood of late. Two small grocery stores and a gas station had been bought up; and in fact it seemed that overnight the community was transitioning. So that Amy knew their first minutes together after the service would be filled with his enthusing pompously about how wonderful it would be to bring these newcomers to the Light – and for Brown's little church to be a beacon in leading the way for others as well.

She watched him, his heart swelling with joy, as he nearly tripped on his way down off the platform, hurrying to give the supposed new converts a warm embrace. In fact, they were not as young as one might think from a distance. And while greeting them effusively, and while others of the congregation still milled about, the pastor nevertheless had to be struck by the hard eyes of the male member of the twosome. 'The Lord would have to do some softening there!'

It wasn't until a week later, though, when the two visitors came back with four more that Amy really lit into him. It was after the service, in the car on the way to a restaurant, and he was positively exulting.

"Did you see that?" he crowed. "Six of them! Last week two and now six! Pretty soon we'll fill the church!"

"Careful what you wish for, Billy Graham!" she snapped, immediately sorry for the sarcasm.

"What. . .?" He reacted as if he'd been struck. He'd been in full flower and was not used to being cut down at such times.

"I'm sorry," she said, reaching to place a hand on his arm. "But Benjamin, these aren't ordinary parishioners, and these aren't ordinary times. These are probably Muslims and they're up to something. They're moving into the neighborhood and, from what I've read, it doesn't just stop there."

He jerked his arm away, interrupting her and strikingly angry. "You've read? You've read?" He was yelling. "That's the problem with the world – all these Monday morning quarterbacks writing endlessly on social media on every imaginable topic – whether they know anything about the Spirit's working or not. And oh by the way, destroying any hope of inter faith rapprochement along the way!"

It was one of the things she detested – his retreating to his pronounced relationship with the Holy Spirit – that because he was a minister, his relationship was stronger and on a different level, and as a result he couldn't be challenged.

"Why do you suppose it is?" she said impudently, unexpectedly, "that more and more churches in their bulletins list the preacher and his wife as co-pastors?"

He stared over at her, for a second taking his eyes off the road, as always taken aback by her quick witted shifting.

"I have no idea," he said, losing the train of his own thought entirely. He steered the car to a parking spot alongside the curb, and she began again.

"In 1965 there were no mosques in the United States," she said, "and now there are a couple of thousand."

"So what?" he said. "The immigration policy has changed."

"Yes," she said, "but the goals of Islam never have. Always, always they've wanted to take over the West, and have been willing to devote centuries to do it."

"Oh right!" he said. "And because we welcome a few Arabs –and we don't even know if they're Muslims – into our service, America's going to be taken over. Please, as they say, give me a break!"

In ensuing services, however, there were more; and it was subtle in a way, methodical, diabolical. Now when the service ended, inevitably several of the head-scarfed women would surround Benjamin Brown as he descended the platform – something Muslim women would typically never do. Which led of course to Benjamin's conjecture that they really were not Muslims, and thus fruit for the picking. He was in fact impressed with their questions on Scriptural issues; while wife Amy was seething at what to her was blatantly transparent.

"Amy, they are seeking!" he enthused. "And I am so gratified to be doing the Lord's work in what I think may be a large way."

"Like a sheep being led to the slaughter," she muttered under her breath.

"Even if they aren't all genuine – and I'm convinced that most of them are – we're still planting seeds and those seeds will not come back void."

"Benjamin," she implored him more than once, "Islam and our Christian faith cannot co-exist!"

"It's not co-existence I'm looking for," he said, exuding confidence. "It's conversions!"

He looked at her, flushed and again very angry. "Sometimes Amy," he said, "you cross the line. You really do! Your role is to be supportive! Not antagonistic!"

"Islam," she went on composedly, almost as if she hadn't heard him, "was birthed in idolatry and superstition. And at every turn, the classical Islam of today is intertwined with demons and omens and amulets. Even their crescent moon, which they display everywhere, is a pagan symbol – the symbol of the Babylonian moon god."

"Oh for crying out loud, Amy!" he shouted again. "Where do you get all this stuff?"

"Well, I read!" she said again sweetly. "I read."

CHAPTER TWO

Pastor Chooses Compromise

It's a difficult time to be a pastor. I say that often to my wife, but I don't believe she's able to grasp the depth and breadth of it. I mean it's not like we're facing martyrdom or anything like that here in the good old US of A. But there are pressures, and one has to walk a tight line.

There are all these interest groups – like the homosexuals and their marriage beliefs and the feminists with their abortions; the Latinos and their demands for amnesty; and the blacks and their never ending calls for reparations. And we're supposed to accord them all such honor and deference in order not to appear "politically incorrect." Like it or not, it can seep in and affect our preaching, particularly if we are not in total agreement. And then, too, there is the need to protect at all cost our tax exempt status, without which very few of us would be able to open our doors.

"Trying to fit this all within the context of the Gospel message is really challenging, and sometimes seems nearly beyond reach. Truthfully, I think it's only because of my kind of 'laissez faire' approach to the Scriptures that I'm able to soldier on in a loving, accepting way – taking note of course that there's a lot of room for interpretation given the passage of thousands of years of time and the advent of all the new technologies. "Going along to get along" is sometimes impugned *but I relate it to the Apostle Paul's dictum in first*

Corinthians, chapter nine - where he speaks of being all things to all people.

"Don't get me wrong! The Scriptures are wonderful and in most cases uplifting; and I use them to inspire. But it's necessary also to be real – to live in the here and now! And perhaps that's why I had such difficulty relating to Mona Harwell's husband Jake – who I can only characterize charitably as a Neanderthal."

–Reverend Benjamin Brown

Like Amy, Jake Harwell also read a lot, though not typically about religious matters. Jake was a history major; and, as his work experience had taken him throughout the West, he'd become inspired by the exploits of Lewis and Clark, the early mountain men/trappers and the Native Americans. Which led him to read voluminously also about the Nation's founders, their writing of the Constitution and what had motivated the Western expansion.

Wandering ever further from beaten paths and with a growing reverential sense, he shot video of bison and bear; antelope, elk and deer; and all manner of creatures in between. Realizing that, as wonderful as it all was, his was just a lingering taste of the *Garden of Eden* West Lewis and Clark had experienced. And the sense of so much lost – of which the vast bison herds were just one example – had colored his view of modern America in general, and hardened his opinions regarding everything from politics and politicians to greed, materialism and morality.

With a nod to a softer protective side, he *had* married an Indiana woman, Mona, who already had three children. She had fooled him with her passionate conversation regarding salvation and religion. But then, as hard reality set in - the realization of the competitive materialism she expected him to instill in those children – he balked. Heretofore, all he'd learned while roaming the West hadn't necessarily crystallized as philosophy. There had been a lot to absorb, and for a while it just simmered and percolated. But now, ultimately, he couldn't act counter to those things he'd come to know. And wife Mona never would understand the depths to which those beliefs had taken hold.

They fought often, then fought more bitterly; so that finally he agreed to go with her to counseling. Given his values, he didn't see it as a way to compromise, but went along hoping rather to pacify. However, Mona's insistence that they seek help from Pastor Benjamin Brown was decidedly *not* a recipe for success.

Everything about their first session pained Jake, starting with Brown's rambling opening prayer in which, in addition to acknowledging God's sovereignty, he pandered, actually incorporating the munificence of the Creation.

Jake Harwell felt the bile rising in his throat. 'Really? Did the little stuff shirt have any conception? Really?'

The preacher lifted his head and opened his dreamy eyes behind rimless spectacles, then began piously. "Now, my brother and sister, let us examine the points of your contention."

And Jake Harwell wanted to throw up.

"Well . . . .?" Pastor Brown cocked his head, the mannerism deliberately *cute*, as neither Jake not Mona were immediately forthcoming. "Mona, why don't you begin," he said.

She brightened as he spoke her name. "Oh," she said, "I'm just so tired of fighting about this!" Her voice rose and her eyes welled up with tears behind pink tinted spectacles. She was dark haired, plump but attractive in light blue blouse and dark skirt. "It seems like we never have enough and Jake just doesn't care!"

"Enough money?" the preacher asked.

"Yes," she nodded, sniffling. "I don't want my – our children going out looking like ragamuffins all the time!"

Brown leaned forward and touched her forearm solicitously. "Ragamuffins?" he repeated with what passed as a chuckle. "I haven't heard that term in a very long time!"

They were sitting around a glass coffee table in the preacher's inner office. And with the focus on the word *ragamuffins*, the mood lifted somewhat – which of course had been Brown's intention.

"Jake," he said, "I know times are tough, but what do you have to say about what Mona just said? And I wonder - have you been tithing?"

To which Jake, who was leaned forward with hands on his knees – a moderately sized man in jeans and faded blue work shirt – jerked his head perceptibly.

"Well," he said, and his voice was deep and gravelly, "before we go any further, I'd like to ask you something, Preacher?"

"Shoot!" Benjamin Brown smiled most affably, pleased to show flexibility, albeit with his usual condescension. "Ask away!"

"Which do you believe is the greatest enemy to Christianity in our country today? Materialism or Islam?"

And for once in his life, the man who made his way by speaking words was momentarily speechless. 'Who was this man dressed in rough clothes, who, he believed, worked as a tree planter for the Forest Service – who was he to ask such a basically intellectual question?'

"Well, I'm not sure either one is a viable threat to Christianity in America," he stammered at last. "But besides that, such a discussion could take us pretty far a field from our purpose in being here – i.e., your domestic situation."

"On the contrary," Jake came back at him immediately, and choosing not to register his wife's displeasure. "They are both mortal enemies of Christianity in America – a one, two punch with materialism softening us up and Islam gathering to score the inevitable knockout."

"Oh Jake, for heaven sakes!" Wife Mona finally erupted. "Can't you ever *just* let it go?"

"No," he shot back, "this *is* what it's about! And how can anyone counsel us who isn't even aware?"

* * * *

Benjamin Brown had had the materialism discussion in even greater depth with Amy – when he'd first started preaching his prosperity message.
"It seems to me that's walking a mighty fine line," she'd said.

"What's that?" he'd said, still flushed with perceived success after preaching the series' first salvo.

"Well, it's as if you're saying that faith in Christ's death for our salvation is not enough and that other work by us is required – which is the very definition of counterfeit religion. Plus, I think that the biggest obstacle to Christ in America is already the worship of mammon, and all the glitz and glamour that it affords. Everywhere you look there are shrines of some sort, whether fancy shopping malls, nightclubs, gambling palaces, or whatever! Not to mention all the new technologies that people are obsessed with owning."

"Oh for goodness sakes, Amy," he'd exploded, truly exasperated with her again. "Did I say anything about worship? No! What I emphasized was the principle of tithing, and God's inevitable blessing on the faithful giver."

"And that's what bothers me," she said. "That word "inevitable." I don't think you can put God in an automatic box like that – because we know from Scripture His ways and thoughts are not ours. And the idea that if people give money, they'll get more money is in itself a limitation on the idea of blessing. He blesses in various ways."

"But he does bless," Brown said, grateful then for the last word and ignoring her sigh as a further commentary.

* * * *

"I can't deny that there's materialism in our culture," he said smoothly, addressing Jake Harwell in his most patronizing fashion. "But it's also true that our capitalist system has generated the wealth that has enabled us to be the greatest *giver* nation the world has ever seen. We have helped more people worldwide than any other country, and that largesse has given our missionaries entrée in many areas that would have been otherwise *verboten*."

Harwell was watching him closely, studying him, it seemed - which made the pastor surprisingly uncomfortable. Then Harwell spoke quietly. "But what about our people here in America?" he asked. "What about our spiritual state, or lack thereof. Shouldn't that be the first priority?"

Benjamin Brown blinked. He was not comfortable with opposition; and, while wife Amy frequently challenged, there was always underneath a certain vexed fondness. Never like this!

"Mister Harwell," he began at length, "I agreed to meet with you folks in the hopes that I might be of help in your situation. I did not, however, volunteer for a debate on theology, nor for verbal abuse."

"I'm sorry if I raised my voice," Jake Harwell said, even more quietly, trying somehow to slide his intensity past his wife's growing displeasure. "I just don't see, though, how we can ever have a fruitful discussion when there is obviously no agreement on the parameters."

"Well, I don't know that we've actually had enough of a back and forth," Pastor Brown intoned, "to establish where parameters might possibly be."

"How much back and forth does there need to be?" Harwell said, now actually getting louder. "Your full on embrace of the prosperity message disqualifies you in my mind from any fair arbitration between Mona and myself. Because our fundamental problems revolve around the driven acquisitiveness of our culture – Mona's embracing of it as the required avenue for her children and my utter rejection of the godless corruption that it's creating."

Pastor Brown leaned forward on the edge of his chair, hands clasped in a prayerful attitude, trying somehow to regain control. "Well, he said, striving to sound upbeat, friendly, "Tell me, Jake, why is it you feel so strongly the way you do? Obviously, it's a problem for your wife, as I dare say it would be for most any American wife. But then, I understand we're all different and we all have different histories."

Harwell glowered at him – started to speak, caught himself, then went ahead, at first restrainedly. "Look," he said, "you and a lot of other preachers, haven't confronted the *real* problems facing our nation and our nation's Christians – which once upon a time were synonymous. The first two presidents, George Washington and John Adams were strong believers; and the framers' strong beliefs are reflected in the Constitution. So that it's no coincidence that both Christianity and the Constitution are under attack now simultaneously. And you guys, instead of standing up and identifying the real problems and rallying the Lord's army, continue to make nice with the church's greatest enemies – mammon and Islam. Christianity cannot co-exist with mammon and Islam. The Bible teaches that so plainly; and yet of course you know better. Oh, it makes me want to throw up!

"Oh, and by the way, Pastor, how should we characterize this church of yours – as closer to the Church of Laodicea, in the Book of Revelations, or the Church at Sardis?"

At which point, Benjamin Brown stood up suddenly – though apologizing. 'He had another session which was imminent,' he said. 'But maybe they could meet again sometime later on.' They all stood up then and had a hasty prayer, holding hands, while Brown prayed the Lord would bring enlightenment and a sparing of their souls.

CHAPTER THREE

Muslim Brotherhood in Hamas, Al-Qaeda, America

In 1987, the Muslim Brotherhood established the Islamic Resistance Movement (Hamas) to destroy Israel; one year later, it assisted in the creation of Al-Qaeda as a "base" for the holy war against the western world. Members of the organization came to include blind sheikh Omar Abdul Rahman, the architect of the 1993 bombing of the World Trade Center; Dr. Ayman al-Zawahri, the founder of the Egyptian Islamic Jihad; Osama bin Laden's chief deputy, Abdullah Azzam, the co-founder of Al-Qaeda; and Khalid Sheikh Mohammed, the mastermind of the 9/11 attacks."

–Paul L. Williams, *Crescent Moon Rising*

(Muslims) must understand that their work in America is a kind of grand jihad in eliminating and destroying the Western civilization from within and sabotaging its miserable house by their hands so that Allah's religion is victorious over all other religions."

–Dr. Mohammed Akram Adlouni
(adopted unanimously – May 22, 1991)
Muslim Brotherhood Planning Council

President Barack Obama has been 'aiding and abetting the enemy" in the fight against terrorism by allowing members of the Muslim Brotherhood into the White House."
–General Paul Vallely
Newsmax Television (February 16, 2015)

Guy Alexander, black journalist for a renowned Washington D.C. newspaper, rolled tiredly out of bed. The early light of dawn was just starting to filter through the translucent beige curtains, and he stumbled off towards the shower with nary a backward glance at his still sleeping blond *male* conquest.

His head was throbbing with a hangover; but far worse than that were the bankrupt feelings that continued to plague him. Something was seriously wrong, which his drink be-clouded mind had been unable to get a handle on for some time now. And in fact, his mind was so often be-clouded these days that he despaired of ever finding an answer. It was, he thought ruefully, perhaps just the *new norm*. And while he thought it might have to do with the Nation's and the government's general malaise – which he covered endlessly – deep down, he knew it was something more.

Later, at the paper, he attended the morning briefing session where new assignments were handed out and progress reports submitted. Also, there was the normal advice about emphasis, and warnings as to areas to be avoided – i.e. guidelines which he increasingly resented, as they'd become ever more tight windowed and specific. When he'd first come to the paper, he'd thought 'well, ok, that's how they do it here in the big leagues.' But the ever greater demands of political correctness were now somewhere between constricting and smothering.

Of course, the money was great and there were plenty of perks. Just the daily access to the country's movers and shakers and the possibility of perhaps influencing policy was a heady mix. But the fact that the paper had gone from government watchdog to an almost blatant partnership with one of the political parties left another discomfort that would not go away.

He'd come up from poverty, benefiting from all the affirmative action programs and was grateful for the access they'd afforded him. However, it was not as if it had been handed to him. He had worked hard, developing his ear for language; graduated from Columbia School of Journalism with honors; and continued to seize at every ensuing opportunity.

Also, along the way, he'd found himself in the company of the *elites* – the Ivy League intellectuals – who are schooled from birth, it seems, that it is their country to run. Period! Fanatically – one might even say, "religiously" – committed to creating a *better world order,* a structured utopia of peace, reasonable prosperity and acceptable ideas. It would be, too, a society of liberality from which the dusty old values of Christianity (those values instilled by his transplanted from the South mother) would be jettisoned summarily, relegated deservedly to the trash heap of history. The fact that they had held sway for so long seemed after all incomprehensible in this (latest) new *age of reason.*

Sometimes this gnawed at him, though decreasingly, as libertine sexuality became ever more enticing. He was after all young, rich and extraordinarily handsome – above average in height, lithe and athletic, mocha skinned, with wonderful warm eyes and an engaging manner. His usual propensity to laugh had reflected an enjoyment of life and women flocked to him to the point where he thought he'd gotten bored.

Sometimes, he'd felt bad for them, as so often they'd read more into the one night stands than actually existed. However, over time, he seemed de-sensitized to that as well; and, in his growing self-analysis, regarded it as just one more troubled circumstance.

This particular day, he attended a hearing on Capitol Hill – a House meeting on Homeland Security, and with the focus on homegrown terrorists. Then afterwards, there was a press conference with Tom Trebekka, the committee chairman. He was a typical *pol,* a stuffed shirt, full of himself Democrat, whom Alexander loathed – probably, he thought, just because of his forever politically correct verbiage.

"Given the rate of immigration, do you foresee that we will soon have "no go" Muslim zones, as they do in Europe?" he asked when it was his turn.

"Negative! Negative! The Administration certainly does not foresee any extensive development along those lines," the florid faced one pontificated. "America after all – as you know – has been and always will be a great *melting pot*. We encourage assimilation in every way possible, and never exclusion. That is why we have free English classes in almost every city; many free community colleges; free counseling for matriculating families; and on and on and on!"

'And on and on and on,' Alexander thought glumly. 'Always on and on and on – to nothing and nothing and nowhere!'

Adhering as usual to the party line, however, in his next day's article, he simply restated the gist of similar pieces of weeks gone by – that there was no elevated terror risk, and that now there'd been several months elapsed since the semblance of any attempt.

Stuck in neutral, he railed at his dead end feelings, his ill treatment of his returning black fiancée Eloise reflecting his dark unease. Bold, brilliant and beautiful, Eloise had been part of a government trade mission to Europe, headquartered in Paris for six months; and, in her absence, he had engaged in a particular round of debauchery. Which had left him spent now to the point that her presence seemed just one more problem to confront.

He couldn't say that he loved her now – that he loved anyone or anything. And in as much as anyone or anything complicated his existence, he was impatient and churlish.

Eloise was hurt. Of course, she was hurt! They'd been close and she'd loved him. She'd thought that he'd loved her, though she admitted to herself that his proposal was as much a product of her strength as it was his own emotion. But now, though she was hurt, that strength was her salvation.

"Look," she said, "let's make this short and sweet! No apologies! No backing and filling! You've moved on to somewhere, or someone, I'm not sure. But I chose to go to Paris; it wasn't your choice. And I realize now that it was a mistake. Or maybe it wasn't. I don't know. But the Lord God does, and in time He'll show me what's next."

"Goodbye, Guy!" she said. And she was gone.

Whereupon afterwards, he felt it – if not grieving to the core, at least troubled by her parting words and most particularly by her reference to God. He hadn't thought of God in a very long time, and no one else he knew even spoke of Him.

He muddled on, relying for a time on alcohol and somehow not comfortable delving into his little black book (or more modernly, the contact list on his cell phone). It all seemed less meaningful than ever, as well as ironic. Here he was a young black man from the sticks, risen to the heights - educated, relatively rich and with some degree of fame – drowning his sorrows in a bottle. What sorrows? He still couldn't even define them.

Finally, he called Eloise and she agreed to meet him for coffee, but only if he promised 'never to get romantic with her again.'

"You look like hell!" She greeted him less than affectionately. "Did you try to drink up the whole ocean?"

He grinned for the first time in awhile, thinking she was more like the big sister he'd never had.

They sat at a back booth in a quiet little café, and finally she got to tell him about her experiences in France. Which in truth were more alarming than uplifting.

"It's not like when I was a little girl and we lived there," she said softly. "France has become unbelievably Muslim. Everywhere there are Muslim mini-states that are off limits. And there's this darkness that seems to permeate everywhere and everything."

"It's going to happen here," he said grimly.

"What?" She said surprised. "What did you say?"

"It's happening here!"

CHAPTER FOUR

Seminaries Say Goodbye to Demons

When wife Amy spoke angrily of Islam and its roots in witchcraft, I have to admit I was somewhat taken aback. In fact, she spoke to me as if she were addressing some small child. After going on about Islam being birthed in superstition and idolatry, and about the enduring symbols - the rising crescent moon (the symbol of the Babylonian moon god) and the yearly Hajj or pilgrimage of millions of people to kiss the mystical black stone of Mecca – and that the classical Islam of today is intertwined with various demons, omens and amulets, she even went on to expound upon the English word genie, which she said has its root in the Arabic word jinni. Throughout the Arabic world, she continued laboriously, jinn are feared as the cause of multiple problems; plus, when extreme troubles arise, the believers summons the services of various fallen angels.

"Well, as I say, the level of nonsense was just breathtaking. "It all sounds like gobble di gook to me," I shot back at her, irritated to be spending any time on it at all. "We're not living in the seventh or eighth century, Amy," I noted. "We're living in the here and now! And you know as well as I do that this is all stuff and nonsense. I happen to believe that most of those who study the Quran modernly – or *what you termed the classical Islamist – are indeed students of their book and eschew all this other rubbish."*

"Which," she retorted, "all sounds very nice and sweet but ignores the inconvenient truth that in reality multiple millions upon millions ultimately adhere to the latter part of their book - which declares that the tormenting and dispatching of the infidel is done in Allah's service. The result of which is that in more and more places there's a resulting spirit of violence leading to chaos and death."

"Well, of course, I'm not going to deny the occurrence of such tragedies," I said, "but I'm not ready to ascribe them to some spirit – the spirit of violence, as you say."

She looked at me for a long moment, obviously measuring her words; then let fly anyway.

"Of course, you wouldn't" she said dismissively. "Your job is to interpret and make understandable the spiritual side; and yet so often you seem to dismiss the spirit world entirely. You preach Jesus and in fact, according to Brother Kyle at my school, about a quarter of all Jesus' miracles had to do with the expelling of Satan and his demons. Nevertheless, you and a lot of other preachers nowadays seem to indicate that this is not a ministry for today. Which of course leads to the question: where did all the demons go? Were they just rolled up in some medieval prayer rug and shipped off to a different century?

"I don't get it, Benjamin! Why is there no deliverance done now? Is the idea just too creepy for you guys? Is that why it's not emphasized in the seminaries? You're afraid? And even though the Scriptures teach that fear is one of the enemy's greatest weapons."

Well, you can see what I was up against - just a daily ration of nonsense, over and over again. So that sometimes, I thought without the Lord's finally intervening, there might never be a real breakthrough. "That's enough, Amy!" I shouted at her. "Absolutely enough!"

–Reverend Benjamin Brown

T he following Sunday after Benjamin's aborted counseling session with the Harwells, Amy made it a point of visiting with the unhappy couple before the start of the service. They were just getting seated towards the rear when she approached; and, while she had had some dealings with Mona at a ladies' retreat, she'd never more than exchanged greetings with husband Jake.

The effect that Jake Harwell and the counselling session had had on her husband the pastor, though, had made her curious. And from Benjamin's whining description, she thought Jake had things to say she wanted to hear.

In fact, given the counselling fiasco, it was surprising that Jake would be there at all; and Amy surmised it must be an indication of his wife's actual sway, or perhaps just his strong ongoing effort to assuage her feelings and somehow make it work.

Tall, slender, blonde and dressed in cheerful springtime yellow, she approached, giving the more conservatively dressed in gray Mona an obligatory hug; then perhaps too quickly turning to Jake.

"Good morning!" was all that she said, but with a kind of knowing twinkle.

And predictably, Jake Harwell noticed.

"Good morning!" he said, doubtless surprised that friendliness should come from that quarter.

"Do you think the Arabic visitors are sincere?" she asked in a lowered voice, besides the immediacy of it, further astonishing with such a question emanating from a pastor's wife.

Jake Harwell even blinked, then after a pause finally managed in a quiet voice of his own. "Oh, they're probably sincere all right," he said. "But sincere in the pursuit of Christ? That would be unusual in the extreme."

She nodded seriously, his quiet intelligence certainly not taking away from her own reservations and suspicions. However, she quickly returned to the wife then, gripping her hand and repeating the ritual "so glad to see you" – before moving on then to greet others of the flock. While Jake Harwell, who merely shrugged at his wife's wondering 'what was that all about?' was nevertheless duly impressed - that at least one of the pastoral team seemed to get it.

At home after the service, Amy once again confronted her *soon to be ex*-husband Pastor Benjamin Brown. He in fact was pouting at her lack of response to still another Sunday sermon. He had poured himself into the preparation, as he ordinarily did, then had focused all energies on the platform - only to find himself afterwards fishing for compliments. At the diner where they'd gone typically afterwards for Sunday brunch, he'd finally asked her directly.

"Well, what did you think?" he said hopefully, like some little puppy dog eager for a bone.

"About what?" she returned brightly, knowing full well what he wanted.

"About the message!" he said vexed. "My message!"

"Well I don't know," she shrugged. "Was it any different?"

"Well probably you wouldn't say that if you'd been listening."

"I was listening! And I am saying it!"

Then he was silent. They both were until finally they were home.

"Look," she said, almost as soon as they were inside the door, "materialism is a false religion, as much as Buddhism, Hinduism or your favorite Islam. And with your quote, unquote *prosperity message,* you're just fueling it. 'Just tithe big and you too will be blessed with trips to Las Vegas or Monte Carlo or Disney World – or whatever other centers of pleasure!"

"Oh for the love of God!" he burst out, really losing it. "That's not what I'm saying at all. And anyway to characterize materialism, i.e. capitalism, as a false religion is a satanic lie in itself. How many times do I have to say it? Satan can't stand capitalism's success because it means that funds will be in abundance for the propagation of the Word!"

"Just more rationalization," she sniffed, "which is what has brought about the dry rot in our churches. Churches send out missionaries all right, but usually now only to *safe zones* – places where there are open invitations. While many of the really difficult demonic controlled zones are generally ignored. It's called *risk avoidance* and is a product, I believe, of your leisure first materialism."

She paused for breath and he stared at her enraged.

"Amy, I don't think you know what you're talking about!" he managed at last. "In fact, I know you don't!"

Nevertheless, she went on, her own ire rising.

"I visited with Jake Harwell today, before the service," she said switching and with a trace of the vindictive. "He was there, you know, and he didn't seem all that unreasonable to me."

"Jake Harwell? Dammit Amy!" He was yelling.

Which only elicited in her a return to her quiet calm.

"Did you say he compared us to the Church at Sardis? Wasn't that the church on top of a cliff somewhere – where they believed they were impregnable to attack?"

He blinked, trying then to regain his composure, while unable to process her calm.

"The Church at Sardis," he said, settling finally on his professorial tone, "is best known for being a dead church."

"I know," she said, "but isn't it also true that they operated under the guise of a false invincibility?"

"I've forgotten. I guess that's true."

"Well," she said, "maybe that's what Mister Harwell was getting at in comparing us to them."

"In what way, Amy?" he asked more gently, the professorial progressing quickly now to conciliatory laced with condescension.

Which immediately rekindled her anger. "In that you believe that the influx of the Muslims is harmless!" she snapped.

Whereupon, he grabbed a book off the table – a Bible in fact – and slung it against the wall.

"I'm not going to hear another word about the Muslims," he bellowed. "Do you understand me, Amy Brown?"

"I understand you perfectly," she said. "And I promise you'll never hear another word about the Muslims from me, or any other word for that matter. And oh, by the way, as of now you can drop the word Brown after Amy!"

"What?" he blinked, as if only just realizing the utter seriousness. "What are you saying?"

"I can't do this anymore," she said simply. "Can't continue to be supportive of a willfully blind buffoon!"

* * * *

It wasn't until the second week after her leaving that members of the congregation began to notice. Behind the scenes, however, the pastor already had been planting seeds – hints of so-called *infidelity* to certain of the more notorious gossiping types. Knowing that Amy had more friends among the faithful than he and seeking to draw sympathy - thus guarding against possible attrition.

And besides that, it continued to be, he thought, an exhilarating time for the church. More and more Muslims were showing up each week – soon up to twenty – and he was increasingly tasking the elders to work with them – *to explain Christ to them*. If they could succeed in this and, if the church continued to grow in that direction, then he thought excitedly that they might become a model, even nationally. He was aware that there was an influx of Mid-Easterners in other parts of the country, and believed it was important in how the Body of Christ should be perceived.

His ideas on the subject grew even more expansive and certainly that was one thing helping him to overcome Amy's loss. There was no denying the empty feeling he encountered on going home at the end of the day – the very emptiness of the house reminding over and over of her brightness of spirit and engaging manner. He even missed their head butting to a certain extent; and, while there was no one he could confide it in, there were surprising times of being so broken that he wept.

Steadfastly, he focused on the work. Then one day, seeming Providentially, he received a surprise visitor to his office. It was the area's Imam; and up to that point Brown hadn't even known there was one. He had mixed feelings, too, at first - actually with a stab of fear that the man was there to protest Brown's stealing members from his Islamic flock.

He was short, swarthy with a trimmed beard, dressed in western coat and slacks. Then immediately, his warm manner set Benjamin at ease. In fact, there was seemingly an instant recognition and respect between them, Brown might have reported to Amy if she were still around - a kind of two men of the cloth *simpatico*.

They sat on facing couches just inside Brown's inner office where so many of his counseling sessions took place. And the Imam – whose name was Abdul Rahmin – was lavish in his praise regarding the church's overall furnishings. Nor was he there to be in any way critical, he assured; he just wished that they become acquainted.

He reported that he'd been in the city for less than a year himself; but then they never got around to discussing more about his situation – whether he, in fact, was leader of a mosque, or anything about his family either. Rather, early on, he brought the conversation around to Benjamin's personals – subtly – having of course learned of Amy's desertion through his spies in the Sunday services.

After which, Pastor Benjamin Brown found himself pouring out his heartbreak, decidedly grateful for the opportunity to share with and confide in another member of the clergy. To the point of even shedding some tears.

The Imam spoke soothing words and even came around the center coffee table, to sit beside Benjamin and place a sympathetic hand on his shoulder. Then later, when the grateful Pastor Brown showed him to the door, he assured him that he'd soon be in touch.

But then afterwards, Benjamin Brown was truly nonplused by the rapidity with which that took place. In fact, the very next day, a young Arab woman showed up, introduced herself as *Haji* and said that the Imam wanted her to help with the household chores until the pastor was *feeling better*. She would come every day for a couple of hours and there would be no charge. And the Imam and she would be much honored, she said, if Brown would accept this as a gift of friendship between their two faiths.

Benjamin Brown was overwhelmed with gratitude – that anyone would care, and especially his new Muslim cleric friend. He wanted to shout for joy! Then actually caught himself wanting to exult to Amy. He accepted the girl's offer gladly and they scheduled the two hours for early afternoons, right after lunch.

She came always in a head scarf with long skirt and long sleeve blouse buttoned chastely at the neck. Slender, light skinned, perhaps twenty years old and barely with a word to say. She would come, do the dishes, make up the bed, straighten the living room and the study. And sometimes, he'd be at the computer, working on an upcoming message, or perhaps holding a counseling session. And in fact, there was so little interaction between them that it was easy to forget she was there at all.

Interestingly, too, after the Imam's visit, the number of Arabs in the congregation increased markedly again, and Brown didn't know how to explain it. It was almost as if the Imam were referring them, though that made no sense whatever. So that, Benjamin just chose to thank the Lord for his burgeoning new ministry, vaguely troubled notwithstanding that some of his old regulars were apparently getting nervous, increasingly absent and perhaps going elsewhere.

Now on a Sunday, there were forty to fifty of the new people in attendance; and, while the church elders had been struggling with assimilation, offering one to one counseling and new convert classes, to date there had not been a single new declaration for Christ. Furthermore, weekly giving was actually down, what with the increasing absence of the old timers and the failure of the newcomers to give anything at all.

"All in good time!" Pastor Benjamin Brown would intone. "All in good time!" Reminding himself often of the virtue of patience.

CHAPTER FIVE

Islam's War with All

Unlike America's political leaders, Muslims do not recognize the legitimacy of all faiths. Their religion according to Bernard Lewis ("The Political Language of Islam") divides the world into two: the House of Islam (dar al-Islam), where Muslims rule and the law of Islam prevails and the House of War (dar ul-Harb), comprising the rest of the world. "Between these two," Lewis writes, "there is a morally necessary, legally and religiously obligatory state of war, until the final triumph of Islam over unbelief."

–Paul L. Williams, *Crescent Moon Rising*

One day, the Imam called on him again and, with that, everything changed. It was an hour or so after lunch and he was in the study, working on a new message on the computer. The girl Haji had arrived and was, he assumed, back in the kitchen doing the dishes. So that hearing the rectory doorbell, he rose to answer it himself.

He opened the door, registering pleased surprise at the appearance of the Imam, extending his hand as his esteemed friend crossed the threshold. But then, an event transpired which seemed impossible – from out of a movie, or a dream sequence – and life afterwards would never be the same. The girl, as it turned out, was not in the back kitchen after all.

Rather, she appeared suddenly in the doorway of the bedroom which, like the study, also opened on the front hallway. And she was clad, not modestly as usual, but now in what Brown recognized dimly as his own cloth bathrobe – which opened wide as she stopped in mid stride, revealing her firm young breasts and very hairy nether region.

Brown sucked in his breath; the Imam managed an *oh!* And the girl retreated quickly back out of sight into the bedroom. However, in that instant, there was really no going back – no, as they say, *putting the tooth paste back into the tube.*

Benjamin Brown was transfixed. 'What could he do? Go ahead and invite the Imam in and try to explain? What should he do?' Panicked, he couldn't even speak. "I . . . . ," he stammered, then stopped.

Whereupon, the Imam stepped forward, supplying the needed leadership – once again resting a hand on Benjamin's now trembling shoulder – rescuing him.

"Let's just go into your study, Benjamin," he said, striding past and leading the way in. Then sat on the couch next to Benjamin as before – paternalistic, calming, reassuring.

"I never . . . ." Benjamin started, but again the Imam stopped him, raising a finger to his lips. And Benjamin realized why this man of such magnetism was a leader of men, the low voice at once calming and supportive. The voice almost mesmerizing in its calmness.

"It's all right, Benjamin!" he said. "It's all right! There is nothing to fear or worry for. Just take a deep breath, then let it all go."

Which Benjamin Brown did, almost as if he *were* being hypnotized – only shortly afterwards to be jerked to the true reality.

"I understand, Benjamin," the Imam said. "We are men and sometimes these things happen."

"But . . . ." Benjamin started but again stopped with a stammer.

"But," the Imam continued, "there is no reason that anyone in your church should ever know about any of this." And he looked into Benjamin's eyes, searching him, Benjamin thought - still not quite understanding.

"Let's just say this thing never happened, Benjamin," he started. "I don't care anything about it, so you shouldn't either. The thing I came here to discuss with you today is a completely different matter."

And Benjamin took another deep breath, striving to clear his mind of what had happened, but continuing to trouble over it. 'What,' he thought, 'was the girl doing now?'

"The girl," he said, starting to get up. "I've got to see what she's doing – have got to get to the bottom of this!"

"Don't bother, Benjamin!" the Imam said, hand back on his shoulder. "She's already gone, I guarantee it – long gone right after she saw me."

"Now Benjamin," he went on, "the reason I'm here is to ask a big favor of you, my dear friend. Are you ready? Focused?"

Benjamin licked his lips. Nodded.

"Benjamin we – my followers – the followers of Allah – are needing a place to worship. There are so many of us now in the neighborhood, and I am asking you in the name of cooperation and ecumenism and multi-culturalism, etc., to share your building with us. Of course, it will remain your church - on Sundays, and the rest of the week; but from Friday night through Saturday night it will serve as our mosque. And I'm sure both our Gods will be pleased with the brotherhood."

Benjamin Brown stared at him, dumbfounded – still not understanding the connection and what had been done to him.

"Oh gosh, I don't know," he stammered. "I'd have to think about it – pray about it. I never considered."

"Well, I understand," the Imam went on smoothly, "lots of things happen which we never consider beforehand. But, we adapt and go on as best we can, don't we?"

He stopped, leaning forward again, looking knowingly into Benjamin's eyes - Pastor Benjamin Brown who continued not to get the full scope of it, thereby embarrassing himself even further.

"Benjamin," the Imam said, beginning to show some vexation at the slow uptake. "My friend, let us remain friends, and I will *never* mention what was seen here today. No one in your congregation will ever know. No rumors will ever be spread. And we will co-exist and cooperate here in this truly wonderful facility."

He rose to leave, reaching down to grasp Benjamin's limp right hand.

"We will be in touch soon, Benjamin," he said. "We'll need to make new signs advertising the building's twin purpose, and how we can best transition the sanctuary from one service to the next."

* * * *

And shortly thereafter, the Imam's pronouncement came to pass. A large new sign was erected with a cross and rising crescent moon depicted side by side; and with the words "multi-cultural center" displayed prominently. While underneath, the mosque hours for Friday night, Saturday and Saturday night were listed alongside Reverend Brown's Sunday morning and Wednesday evening service times.

In order for Muslims to unroll their prayer rugs, pews were removed each Friday afternoon from the sanctuary into the adjoining rec center, then returned early Sunday mornings. But while members of Brown's congregation were always present on Fridays, in fact to take the lead in the labor, nevertheless on Sunday mornings they were inevitably the *only* workers present. Which of course led to bruised feelings, with the Christian men wondering why Pastor Brown didn't lobby for the Arab men's help on Sunday mornings, naturally not understanding Benjamin Brown's position of zero leverage.

In fact, too, Pastor Brown's congregation was soon melting away at an increasing rate. Of course, his much cherished fifty or so Arab types disappeared immediately, then re-appeared right afterwards in the Imam's Saturday mosque. But then, even with them gone, the remaining Christians – the actual Christians – grew restive, not comfortable with the shared building and of course seeking alternatives. The city had numerous other Christian churches, most of which were in neighborhoods not (yet) overrun with Islamists; while there was now in their own church a different feeling entirely – one described by an older Pentecostal type as an "unwelcoming spirit." Which of course was a term rejected by that modern day theologian and thinker, Pastor Benjamin Brown.

Contributions were drying up, though, and before too long, Pastor Brown was to the point where he could no longer make his half of the mortgage payment – a 50-50 sharing which the Imam had agreed to only grudgingly anyway, what with the church being in Benjamin's hands six of the week's seven days and the living quarters continually. Thus, when Benjamin couldn't come up with the money, mercy was also in short supply. Henceforth, the mosque would make the full payment, the Imam stated; but Benjamin, and what was left of his flock, would have to be on their way.

Thus, barely six months after wife Amy's departure, Benjamin Brown found himself out on the street as well.

CHAPTER SIX

Europe's Islamic Invasion

I am defending and protecting this country that we've built up over five, six centuries. What we now have here, goddamn it, is a kind of fifth column. People who are capable of destroying and depleting this country.... I have no desire to defend their interests. That is why I tell them: you can stay here in this country, but you have to adapt....

"I refuse to hear repeatedly that Allah is great, almighty and powerful, and I am a dirty pig. "You are a Christian dog, an infidel." That's what they shout! And you accept this and keep silent. Until now I've been very calm and disciplined. I never spoke like this before. But you've made yourselves their doormats. You've let yourselves be bullied by them. I'm not with you anymore....Because the people of this country are fed up and don't accept so-called political correctness any more....

"If I have to choose my words more carefully, that's fine with me. But this is about the future of your children and grandchildren; it touches everything I strive for. There is no other issue.... If I must be silenced or eliminated, I accept that fate. But the problem and the threat will not disappear....The people are sick of it, knowing what is going on ....

*"The police are invisible – they do nothing about it.
And if you have the courage to tell them, they'll tell you right to
your face you're discriminating."*

–Pim Fortuyn
Dutch Politician (assassinated)
Address to Party Leaders, February 2002

Soon after Amy divorced Benjamin Brown, she went away to Europe. Her mother was Dutch, had come to the States as a young girl and had related enough pleasant memories that Amy had always been curious. Also, as neither her mother nor father had ever approved particularly of Benjamin Brown, they were not heartbroken at the breakup. In fact, when Amy first broached the trip to Holland, they were quick to volunteer help. They were not poor, after all, and her father entrusted her with a credit card and the gentle warning that she just 'not go crazy.' So that, Amy departed then with a new life on her mind.

She was met by her great aunt Helena at the Amsterdam airport – to be charmed right afterwards by the laid out roads; walkways and bicycle lanes; the intricate system of canals and dikes and interesting preserved old houses. She was thrilled with the proliferation of bicycles and people riding seemingly everywhere, along with a relative absence of cars and the acceptable practices of going places on foot, by boat and sometimes by rail. And in fact, she reveled at the reliving of some of her mother's fond memories.

Aunt Helena was gray haired, rosy cheeked, plump and hearty; married to Harald, a slight, dark bearded and very quiet Norwegian. Together, they'd raised two sons, who were both now living in Norway and whom, Helena declared, she and Harald expected to be joining in the near future. And while Amy didn't ask why at first - merely assuming them not wanting to continue living apart - after having stayed for several months, she better understood.

Her aunt did much to make her feel at home, escorting her to many of the places her mother had enjoyed, visiting her old schools and the university; strolling by the canals and several times cruising them on boats; lingering in the seemingly endless museums and riding bicycles in a nearby park. However, those times when they went further afield – heading outside the city's limits by car or train – they would pass through seemingly miles of run down suburbs. There, there were rows and rows of shabby, hopeless appearing apartment buildings with teeming Arab populations. Neighborhoods where Harald would never stop the car, and where Arab mothers, wrapped head to toe in dark burqas, seemed always out pushing baby strollers in the midst of swarming other children.

Of course, Amy had known something of Europe's growing Muslim population, but now she realized that simply reading about it did not do it justice. Now, she was startled by the magnitude and naturally, too, was reminded of the unease she'd felt with Benjamin Brown's unfolding experience.

In the beginning, too, she'd asked what she thought was a rather inane question – something to the effect of 'do all Muslims live in these areas?' But it was a question which nevertheless drew an immediate chill and tight lipped response.

"Not all!" her aunt said. Which in fact ended the discussion for the time.

Still, back inside her hosts' small, but tastefully furnished home, she was soon intrigued by a large, framed black and white picture in the den. It was a portrait of a beautiful woman of color, whose eyes were warm and strikingly wise; and Amy noticed, also, that down in the right hand corner, the picture had been signed.

"To my friends," it said, "love you always, Ayaan."

So that soon afterwards, one morning when Harald was off somewhere and Amy and Helena were home having coffee, Amy asked. "Who is that, Auntie, whose picture is in the den?" At which point, the true education phase of Amy's trip began.

"That," her aunt replied, "is the very great and very brave Ayaan Hirsi Ali. She is not just our friend; she is a patriot and a friend to the world – though much of the world, and particularly the Muslim world wants her to be dead!'

After which, a torrent of words poured forth from the older woman; and Amy, bright as she was, was overwhelmed, sitting forward in rapt attention, with not only the European situation becoming clearer, but also what she'd witnessed back home as well.

"Multi-culturalism!" her aunt almost spat the words. "It starts with multi-culturalism, the damn fool idea of our elitist educators - our so-called *great thinkers* – and correspondingly stupid politicians. They decided that instead of encouraging our immigrants to assimilate into our culture – and because of the declining birth rate, the Lord knows we were needing immigrants from somewhere – the Muslims were encouraged essentially to keep separate and insulated in their old ways. In effect, so that they wouldn't *become us*, but rather would contribute a spicy new element to our society, complete with interesting cuisine, customs and dress. Given the Muslims' general contempt for the Infidel, however, this strategy has totally backfired. And now we have created in effect a fast multiplying foe which is rapidly overtaking us!" Seven of our city's fifteen districts are now majority, or near majority Muslim, with Schilderswijk – which is referred to locally as "*the sharia triangle*" - having a full 90 percent."

Afterwards, Amy had coffee with her aunt every morning; and nearly every morning Helena would resume with her teaching. Sometimes, Harald would join in as well and, together, they laid out for Amy the shocking Islamization of Europe, and perhaps ultimately the world.

"It will be hard for you to understand this, Amy," Harald said sometime later, repeating some of what her aunt had already told her, but reinforcing the importance in Amy's mind. "You Americans have been a land of immigrants and have reveled in the idea of being what you have deemed a *melting pot*. From this melting pot, migrant families have emerged as true Americans, with shared language, work ethic and culture. And I think Americans may be disbelieving that we Europeans fall far short of that ideal.

"Instead here we have a profound discomfort with the idea of others becoming ourselves – which has resulted in this conscious policy of integration, but with maintenance of original identity. Which, in fact, has enabled the Muslims – who didn't want to be assimilated anyhow – to establish virtual mini-states here, just as in the rest of Europe. And the ridiculous irony is that not only have we admitted huge numbers of immigrants, but have actually encouraged their separation by funding their schools, mosques and community centers. And these are now systematically teaching our demise and overthrow. They, in fact, are people who absolutely despise our western ideals of freedom, pluralism and sexual equality and treat our infidel law as a great big joke."

"Nor do the immigrant Muslim children assimilate either," her aunt said, picking up the thread. "Since they have their own schools, it's only natural for them to continue on with their parents' values. Girls continue to be trained in total submission; and boys to be belligerent and with total authority over women – believing themselves superior to infidels in every way, with neither police, nor politicians, nor other government officials acknowledged to having authority over them whatsoever."

"Increasingly these young men roam Europe in marauding gangs," Harald added, "and our feckless governments exercise a continuing double standard of non-punishment, as it is after all *politically incorrect* for discipline to appear in any way racist, or ethnically based."

"The woman you asked about, Amy," her aunt said one day, "Ayaan Hirsi Ali – whose picture is there on our wall and who at one time honored our house with her presence – is one who has risked her life to speak out against our suicidal government policies, and she with a Muslim background at that!"

They were having coffee this time in the den, and Amy stood up to once again approach the portrait, staring again at the knowing eyes.

"She was born in Somalia," her aunt went on, "and literally escaped from Islam – but not before enduring female genital mutilation, a proposed arranged marriage with an unknown someone in Canada, and assorted other male threats and brutalities.

"Finally, she arrived here and, through a series of events and her own hard work and struggles, she became a co-movie producer with Theo van Gogh, who you may know butchered by a Muslim on an Amsterdam street. Together, she and Theo had produced a movie entitled, "Submission" – which was in fact a film depicting Muslim women's horrific treatment at the hands of Muslim men. And after van Gogh's death and repeated threats on her own life, Ayaan continued to espouse an unflinching defense of democracy, along with blunt criticism for Dutch passivity in the face of fundamental Islam. Which led her finally, surprisingly, to a seat in our House of Parliament – a seat held tenuously at best, as part of her time had to be spent in your country, hiding from the continuing threats on her life."

"Auntie, where is she today?"

"Again in America, sad to say."

"Aunt Helena, I'd heard of female circumcision, but I thought it was only done in Africa. Is it carried on in other places? Surely it's not done here."

"Oh dear!" the older woman replied. "It is done here, and wherever there are Muslims. Because, as I said, they don't assimilate. They *never* give up their culture! And that, in fact, has been the driving force in what I will call Ayaan Hirsi Ali's ministry – her absolute passion to protect young women from what she had to endure. She told us that somewhere in the neighborhood of 125 million Muslim women have undergone this insane brutality.

"First and foremost, of course, is the forced removal of the clitoris, often with something like a rusty razor blade. Followed by a stitching up of the vagina to the size of a pinhead – which protects virginity all right, but results usually in lifelong physical pain, chronic infection and terrible discomfort urinating and in having sex."

Helena stopped then for a moment, unable to say more, an older gray haired lady with tears in her eyes. So that Amy waited until after she'd dabbed at her eyes with a handkerchief.

"And what else, Aunt Helena?" she asked finally, gently. "You said first and foremost. What else was Miss Ayaan fighting for?"

"Oh," her aunt managed, clearing her throat, "she fought against the terrible beatings routinely administered to the Muslim women by the men; the arranged marriages in which women have no say so in whom they will marry; and, worst of all, the honor killings."

"Honor killings?" Amy was blank. Then afterwards – after the explanation – was radicalized herself. Revolted as never before – filled up with it – feeling she had to do something. Anything!

"It is the idea," her aunt said, "that women are subject to the will and authority of men – period! And a woman who goes outside of those boundaries or defies male authority is seen as staining the family's honor and may very well be put to death. And this is particularly true if her disobedience is committed in public. Then the family may consider her dispatch through a so-called *honor killing* as a sacred obligation."

Amy stared at her. "Her own family?"

"You bet," her aunt returned, animated. "Generally at the hand of her father, or perhaps an uncle.

"Come Amy, I want to show you something," she said, leading the way from the kitchen back into the den. She pulled out what appeared to be a leather-bound scrapbook from a desk drawer; then, taking a deep breath, opened it almost reluctantly, with what Amy registered as reverence.

"These are Muslim honor killings which have been reported in the press," her aunt said, turning the pages slowly, "though there are many others that are suspected, but not verified. Ayaan says there are something like five thousand every year worldwide.

"Now throughout Europe, so many of the Muslim areas are labeled as *no-go zones* – virtual mini-states - where even police and firemen don't go, and where only their own *sharia* courts preside that it's impossible to know precisely. Impossible to know just how many bodies they've actually buried.

"Women can be gang raped by others as punishment for something the men in their families have done – to be murdered afterwards by the family men to dispel the shame of the rape. Some young girls are murdered for things they're alleged to have done while on sojourns abroad. Girls have been killed for simply going places with boys unchaperoned; and, under *sharia* law, infidelity and homosexual activities are similarly punished."

Amy leaned over the desk then, reading the news accounts which aligned precisely with her aunt's description. She turned the plastic coated pages slowly, soon lost in thought. She read about a Swedish Muslim woman, Fadine, murdered by her father after refusing to submit to a forced marriage. About Sahjda in Birmingham, England, who was stabbed to death in her wedding dress by a cousin for marrying a divorced man. A sixteen year old London girl, Heshu, whose throat was slit by her father for falling in love with a seventeen year old Lebanese Christian boy,

And there were more: a young woman in Britain killed by her family because *she* had been raped. And an English Muslim girl murdered by her Pakistani father because an unknown boyfriend dedicated a love song to her on a Pakistani language radio station.

Amy stayed for a long time, bent forward and seemingly transfixed, perhaps trying to memorize the details. Then finally as she straightened up, there was a marked change in her demeanor, and a dampening, if not an actual killing, of her light and airy spirit.

"It's monstrous, Aunt Helena!" she said in a low choking voice. "They're monsters! Right out of the seventh century or somewhere!" And she began to cry.

Not many days afterwards then, she felt the need to go home. Harald and Helena drove her to the airport, each with parting thoughts for her that also penetrated into her future.

"I'm sure you're going to encounter more of this in America," Helena said, "and increasingly so. And Americans must understand that wherever these people go, it is never their intention to change and fit in. No, rather it is their driving dream and desire to establish a worldwide caliphate – that we all be governed ultimately and exclusively by *sharia law,* the law of the Quran. And even the most locally successful of them believe that loyalty to their global community – the worldwide community of Islam – supersedes all local civic obligation. Always!

"It is a vast clan, too," Harald added, "with branches in the individual's homeland, as well as in Europe and the United States and everywhere. And remember, also, that the power of their leaders – the imams – is absolute. Thus, even if individuals should want to put civic duty first, fear of the imams and the possibility of sudden death is a dark and real deterrent."

Amy listened soberly, continued depressed - though grateful for the painful counsel nevertheless. Then in the terminal, and just before her boarding, Harald left her with his final thought, which touched on her past with Benjamin Brown as well.

"Dear Amy," he said, grasping both of her hands, "the most important thing is that Europeans have been led to abandon Christianity and, without our Lord as base, the door has been left wide open. Without our Lord, there is no meaningful purpose and, certainly now with the absence of faith, there is no courage. The Muslims at this time have much deeper conviction and commitment; and, without courageous opposition, they will be neither stopped, nor even challenged."

CHAPTER SEVEN

Saudis Writing American Curriculum

Harvard is one of 18 universities which receive government funding under Title VI of the Higher Education Act of 1965. To qualify for that funding, the universities are required to conduct outreach to K-12 teachers, helping them to shape lessons for school children. Elementary and secondary teachers have taken full advantage of the arrangement; after all, they believe they're getting expert insight on Islam and the Middle East from distinguished university scholars. . . . . However, Saudi Arabia has donated millions of dollars to Middle East Centers at universities that receive Title VI funding. The Harvard Middle Eastern Studies Center, author of lesson plans for K-12 history teachers, received $20 million from Saudi Prince Alwaleed bin Talal in 2005, as did Georgetown University, another Title VI recipient. And it's through these Title VI university centers that Saudi funded materials have found their way into K-12 classrooms."

– "Public Schools Teach the ABC's of Islam"
"The Watchman" – CBN News – May 1, 2012

An expert on Islam explains that schools across the United States have implemented radical curriculum in public schools.

Brigitte Gabriel, founder of ACT! For America, explains that students are required to become a Muslim for three weeks, adopt Muslim names, memorize verses from the Quran and visit a mosque for a field trip. Students in these programs, laments the conservative activist, must also recite the Islamic prayer for salvation, which describes Islam as a straight path to God – and Christianity in error."

"Here's what they're teaching in the public schools; what they're telling the students they have to memorize and recite," she says: "Praise be to Allah, Lord of Creation, the compassionate, the merciful, king of judgment day You alone we worship, and to you alone we pray for help."

–American Family Association
"Islamic Indoctrination in the Public Schools"
OneNewsNow.com February 15, 2015

It was, Guy Alexander realized after his talk with Eloise, what was at the heart of his problem – what was really eating at him. Early during Eloise's sojourn in Paris, Guy had been assigned to do a story on CIA involvement in the shipment of weapons to the *mujahadeen* in Afghanistan – back before 9/11 when Osama bin Laden was ostensibly our friend. And while it was old news now, nevertheless it was still interesting; and besides it was the obligatory time of year for liberal media members to once again bash the CIA.

So Guy had gone out, a good soldier, pursuing the story. Then was surprised – really surprised – where the story took him. He soon learned that the Masjid al-Farooq Mosque's al Kitah Refugee Center in Brooklyn had not only been a front for Al-Qaeda, but also for the CIA, shipping funds, weapons and recruits to the anti-Soviet mujahadeen, while in return receiving $2 million annually from the Reagan Administration. And everyday, as his curiosity was further piqued, the single story evolved into what became an obsessive hobby.

Somewhere in the back of his mind had come the decision to research the entire Islamic movement in the United States, as somehow the antics and buffoonery of such home grown actors as Elijah Muhammad and Louis Farrakhan never squared with the deadly serious activities of Masjid al-Farooq and the like. The fact that the founder of al-Farooq – Abdullah Azzam – had been an Osama bin Laden mentor, plus the fact that the notorious blind sheikh Omar Abdel Rahman had been an imam at the Brooklyn mosque at the same time only propelled Alexander further.

Alexander then read rapaciously – everything he could get his hands on. He read Paul L. Williams' *Crescent Moon Rising;* Bruce Bawer's *While Europe Slept;* and Ayaan Hirsi Ali's two books, *Infidel* and *Heretic.*

The Nation of Islam (NOI) had started, he found out, as a simple American con, perpetrated on the streets of Newark by home grown hustlers, Timothy Drew –aka Noble Drew Ali; David Ford-el auk; Master Fard Muhammed; and eventually, Elijah Poole – aka Elijah Muhammad. They preached to African Americans that they in fact were the lost race of Moabites; sold them all new names and identity cards, not to mention red fez, yellow pantaloons, girdles, robes and curled slippers. Then taught straight-faced that a Japanese mother plane with attendant flying saucers had been invented to return all black men to Mecca, and that hated whites would soon disappear from the face of the earth altogether.

Of course, members weren't instructed on the five pillars of Islam, since the instructors themselves had no such knowledge. They *were* told that Mohammed was a black prophet, despite the fact that in reality Mohammed had had an avowed contempt for black people. And further, while in traditional Islam, Mohammed is recognized as Allah's last prophet, both Drew and Poole declared themselves to be prophets, while Fard went so far as to declare himself to be Allah.

Aside from the nonsense and various infighting between the principals and their subordinates, however, the most important thing to emerge from the Nation of Islam's early roots was the markedly racist nature – the deliberate pandering to hatred in a racially charged time, i.e. the preaching of jihad to thousands of blacks in Detroit and Chicago and the formation of paramilitary units and the execution of the first jihads on American soil. At one point, in fact, it was deemed desirable to kill whites (devils) randomly, and with a sliding point scale instituted for men, women and children.

It was not until the ascendancy of Malcolm Little, aka Malcolm X, a former pimp and petty crook, however, that the Muslim Middle East began to take notice of the rage that was burning in so many African Americans. After Malcolm X broke away from the Nation of Islam and established two other groups, he actually made a hajj (pilgrimage) to Mecca where he and the Saudis were mutually amazed – he in actually encountering the five pillars of Islam, and the Saudis in encountering an American who claimed to be a Muslim.

Embraced then as a Sunni convert, Malcolm was feted by excited locals who extended to him and his groups back home twenty-five scholarships to study Islam properly and become bona fide imams. While promising to build a multimillion dollar mosque for him in Los Angeles as well.

So that then, Malcolm X went home, flushed with success – only to be immediately murdered in his Queens, New York home. NOI leaders were suspected – because of deep rooted jealousies; however, none were ever convicted. And regardless, the state of Islam in America was altered forever.

Not long afterwards, U.S. immigration law was changed radically; and, with the passage of the Hart-Cellar Act, over the next several decades, a torrent of traditional Muslims flooded into the country, establishing hundreds and then a couple of thousand mosques nationwide.

The sheer number of mosques established was, in fact, Guy Alexander's greatest surprise; that and the 70 BILLION dollars invested in their building by the Saudis. Obviously, they were finding the U.S. fruitful ground for evangelizing, and were thus much encouraged in achieving their new ultimate goal of converting America to *sharia* law. Further, the violent jihadist activities of some of the mosques left little doubt that, in striving for that goal, the dark side of Islam would be applied whenever and wherever necessary.

Guy noted that the activities of certain of the mosques stood out in particular. For example, Bridgeview Mosque in Chicago had raised millions of dollars for three different terror groups; while the Best Street Complex in Buffalo was known for its actual training of jihadists. Perhaps most troubling of all, though, was Dar Al Hirah Mosque in Falls Church, Virginia, which could boast that several of its founding members were also members of the Muslim Brotherhood – that they'd become known as conduits of funds to Al-Qaeda and Hamas. Also, that one of their leaders, Anwar al Awlaki, in addition to being the first imam to conduct a prayer service at the U.S. Capitol, was also guru to the two hijackers who flew the plane into the Pentagon on 9/11; was a lecturer in classes attended by Major Hasan of the Fort Hood shooting massacre; and became an Al-Qaeda regional commander involved in the London subway bombing; the Times Square attempt; the Little Rock recruiter killing and the *underwear bomber's* fortuitous failing.

And for Guy Alexander, it all piled up, causing a growing perplexity and the question 'why were Americans being kept in the dark about the apparent overall scheme? Why were these events being reported in drips and drabs and never put together in a big picture overview. And who really owned and ran what?'

Afterwards, when he learned about Saudi Arabia manipulating Title VI of the US Higher Education Act, so that millions of dollars could be injected to control the K-12 curriculum in many States, he thought he was already living in a parallel universe. In fact, he learned that with typical stealth, the Saudi government had donated extensively to Middle East Centers at Harvard and the 18 universities which received government funding for conducting outreach to K-12 teachers. And with this bought and paid for influence, the Saudis were enabled to funnel materials directly into American classrooms.

On Christian radio, there were always outrageous stories of Christian suppression in schools – i.e., children suspended for unforgivable speech such as, "God bless you" in response to other kids' sneezing. But now, these tales were juxtaposed with instances of Islam being promoted – with curriculum including weeks of actual study of Islamic customs and dress and, even more ominously, the required memorization of sections of the Quran. 'Where was the much heralded separation of church and state in that?' Christian deejays wanted to know. And while he was not a frequent listener of Christian radio – only dipping in occasionally – references to Title VI set Alexander off on a new round of research.

His discovery that in many instances kids were being required to recite what amounted to an Islamic prayer of conversion – a recitation regarded as being a conversion in Allah's eyes – left him feeling uncomfortable and, as a journalist, unclean. The fact that the President of the United States had made the recent statement that America was now the most populous Muslim nation on earth had raised eyebrows, but of course no direct media challenge. And now with the understanding of the conversion school prayer, Alexander suddenly realized the basis for the Commander In Chief's claim.

He researched and researched, finally putting it all together as best he could. Then, was squelched by his editor; and still didn't understand why.

* * * *

Then, he was not just troubled by the suppression of his story on Islam, but also with other government stories he was instructed to cover as well. Which was soon reflected in his conversations with other journalists.

Tom Reynolds, ace reporter for the *Post* was a tall, balding, gray headed man known for his pungent wit. As they stood at the bar in a little bistro near the Capitol, Reynolds was typically lambasting Catholics – Christian bashing being in fact one of his favorite pastimes.

"So here's *el papa* - the pope – running around the Philippines where every other person is about six years old, telling them they shouldn't be breeding like rabbits. After which, of course, a Vatican apologist scurries forth to assure the world that this didn't in any way signal a change on the policy of birth control, or lack thereof."

"Yeah, I saw that." Guy Alexander replied absently, his mind obviously somewhere else.

"But, you know," Reynolds went on undeterred by Guy's distance, and probably not caring anyway, "if Catholics can still believe in the pontiff's infallibility here in the twenty-first century, I suppose they can also believe in some sort of psychic birth control. However, it would seem this pope – a reputedly educated man – would be aware that such has never worked well to date."

Finally, Guy Alexander took the bait. "Speaking of archaic," he said, "let's talk about your buddies, the Muslims and their seventh century honor killings. A guy's daughter gets raped and so *he* is duty bound to cut her head off, for God's sake! To remove the stain from the family honor!"

"Oh man, Alexander!" his friend replied. "Sorry, I didn't know you were a Christian and that I was offending your sensibilities. Had no idea you believed in such stuff!"

"Look, I'm not a Christian," Guy Alexander replied, strangely aware that he nearly choked on his words – having nevertheless not set foot in a church since he was eighteen years old and gone off for his elitist Ivy League training and secular humanist mind scrubbing. "But let's be fair. "And isn't that what we journalists are supposed to be? Fair? Why are we always bashing the one for what we deem as archaic ideas - albeit relatively harmless ideas - while lauding the other which features acts of the most horrific nature? How is that fair? And where is all this headed?"

Reynolds looked at him for a moment, measuringly; then spoke finally in a false Irish brogue. "Aw Guy, me boy, you have asked a question which is well above our grade of pay. You must try and settle yourself!"

At the time, Guy was assigned to a story on illegal immigration at the Mexican border, where illegal Hispanics and others were pouring across with limited and ineffective opposition – a situation undeniably fostered by the actions and inactions of the Administration. The Democratic Party line, though – and of course the line that Guy was expected to follow – was that the Republicans were responsible. And so naturally, he wrote the story accordingly, emphasizing the suffering of the incoming, while minimizing effects on citizens of the Homeland.

Still, in working on the piece, and particularly after an interview with the Director of Homeland Security – whom Tom Reynolds had labeled as 'that pant load" – he could not escape the idea dogging him that the whole Hispanic illegal immigrant question was being used now as a devious smokescreen.

"What do you hear" he asked Reynolds, "about the *special hardship* Muslims being admitted this year? How many of them are they letting in?"

"Oh man, I'm not sure. Seems to me I heard it's in the hundreds of thousands though."

Guy whistled. "Wow, that many?"

"Well yeah! You know the President's a Muslim himself – or was raised that way. So, we know which way he's going to lean."

"Lean is one thing."

"Meaning?"

"I don't know, man! I don't know."

* * * *

Every day, the foreboding and dread increased, though he still was unable to put it all together, feeling every story he worked to be somehow a piece of a vast, dark, undisclosed plan. 'Who was really running things?' he kept asking himself. 'And what was their end game?'

Soon, he was assigned to cover race riots outside St. Louis along with two other reporters, Fred Corcoran and Jill Donahue – people he'd worked with before and knew and trusted. It was an old news story – white policeman shoots black man and locals – fueled typically by paid agitators from the outside – go on a crazed burning and looting rampage. To be followed in short order by similar out of control sympathy demonstrations in, among other places, Seattle, Chicago and New York.

And Guy Alexander thought the increasing frequency of such events smacked of central planning from somewhere, as it was possible and even probable to observe repeating faces among the demonstrators regardless the city. Increasingly on guard in respect to Islam, he wondered if they in fact were Nation of Islam (NOI) radicals bent on bringing down everything. But then, he was rebuffed at every turn in his efforts to conduct on the scene interviews.

"Get out of the way, mother f_ _ _ _ _," were words he heard quite often. And very little else.

His compatriots, Corcoran and Donahue fared similarly. Like him they were black; and he thought a white reporter wouldn't have lasted two minutes there unless accompanied by a TV cameraman and coveted enhanced exposure. And often, he wondered why the newspaper didn't send a bogus video man out with them, too, just to provide the additional entrée.

At any rate, though, fire bombings and lootings were ugly and unsettling, especially up close and personal. And trying to unwind afterwards, sipping drinks in a hotel bar miles from the scene and naturally comparing notes, the three brought forth from differing viewpoints and experiences. Which led Guy Alexander to a new conjecture that made him physically sick.

'What if it were an orchestrated lead up to the cancellation of the next year's presidential election? A declaration of martial law in which enemies of the state – or enemies of Islam – or both – were rounded up and incarcerated?' And bizarre as the idea seemed at first, certain things like ever increasing surveillance by the NSA (of phone calls, text messages, e-mails and social media entries), plus the heretofore unexplained construction of vast FEMA camps contributed to a growing sense of validity. If there were enough riots in enough places, the President – who had already shown himself quite willing and capable of assuming dictatorial powers - could act unilaterally.

"But that wouldn't be constitutional!" Jill Donahue whined as – a little bit tipsy – he'd put forth his hypothesis.

"Constitutional! Come on, Jill!" Fred Corcoran shot back. "When was the last time any of us fell back on that old saw? Haven't we all believed from Harvard on – and you were there with me, and Guy at Columbia – that the Constitution is a *living, breathing document* – one to be adjusted accordingly with each new generation's changing ways?"

"So, I guess," Guy pressed on grimly, "we really do need to be careful about what we write – if we want to stay on the right side of internment camp gates."

"Oh yeah," Fred Corcoran returned, still not completely convinced and half kidding, "and be willing to swear allegiance to Allah and *sharia* law as well."

"Hmph! Count me out on that!" Jill Donahue sniffed.

"Count you out! Count you out!" Corcoran's voice rose suddenly, as he perhaps flashed back on his radical feminist ex-wife. "Sister, how about if you just close your mouth and drop that veil over your once upon a time lovely face! Because the era of the woman is on the way out!"

In the morning, Guy tried to put their conversation behind. 'Just a product of exhaustion, booze and silliness,' he told himself. And in general, everything seemed normal. America went on. People went to work; cars zoomed up and down the highways; trucks and trains rolled and planes flew. But deep inside, the country wasn't the same; and deep inside his own being, Guy Alexander knew it now - knew that the machinations were underway and well along which would turn things upside down for everyone. Forever!

CHAPTER EIGHT

Political Correctness Killing Free Speech: Muslims Killing Christians!

"As in Europe, Islamists are riding the wave of political correctness – a false religion of diversity killing and first amendment free speech."

"Instilled by professors; preached by politicians, journalists and even preachers; political correctness is national suicide."

"The Peaceful Religion! Muslims beheading, crucifying and stoning children for being Christians. How long before it happens near you?"

–Jake Harwell,
Twitter Account

When he was a young guy, Jake Harwell had helped pay for college by working construction in the summers, the last year tying steel on a huge parking garage project. Workmen using *tie wire* connected steel re-enforcing rods together prior to the cement pouring of foundations and walls; and Harwell became fast and proficient at it. Because the work was repetitive and relatively easy, too, there was inevitable conversation; and sometimes Jake would find himself working alongside a young Muslim from the Sultanate of Oman.

Muhammed was also young like Jake, working more, Harwell surmised, for just the experience rather than need. Each morning before work – at six o'clock – he would unroll his prayer rug right at the edge of the job site, face to the East and proceed through what appeared to be a series of calisthenics, all the while chanting barely audible incantations. And while at first other workers would nudge each other and snicker, even at that time comments were avoided as being politically incorrect.

From their conversations, Jake learned that Muhammed was also a college student, sent to America by his government to add a prestigious western education to his resume. However, during their frequent talks, his tone was always one of condescending teacher rather than fellow student. Still, while Jake often resented the patronizing attitude, nevertheless the Arab's words resonated down through the ensuing years.

"You know, Jake, your country's pre-occupation with material things is troubling."

"Oh?"

He was tall, slender, fine-featured – though dressed similarly to other workmen in t-shirt and jeans, never seeming exactly comfortable. And it was easy to visualize him in traditional snow white *dish-dash*, doubtless a member of his country's royalty.

"Well, I'm not saying that you don't have a wonderful standard of living. Most everyone here has treasures, or dreams of treasures – treasures that are attainable. And it's wonderful, and a wonderful way to live. But I worry that other things are being left out and lost."

"What other things?"

"Well . . . if I might. There is no place for Allah. And in the end, life without Allah is no life at all. That is why we would like to help you."

"Allah? Who is Allah? We don't have Allah here," Jake Harwell replied, at that point missing the larger picture.

Typically agnostic in his youth, though feeling a certain unexplained tenderness and defensiveness for things Christian. "We have churches here," he said. "Plenty of them!"

"Yes, but you don't have what you need most – what all people need – and that is Allah! And all of your material riches will never fill that emptiness."

Years later, when pastors like Benjamin Brown stressed and, to some extent, glorified that prosperity, Jake would be reminded – knowing, however, that it was not a problem of Allah's being missing, but of the missing Lord Jesus Christ. Recognizing a certain godlessness in many of the churches which, when opposed to his deeply spiritual experiences in the outdoors, resulted in an insolvable puzzle for wife Mona. When they finally split, he thought, too, that one of his greatest regrets was his failure to convey to her children the love and appreciation for the Lord's works which he'd learned. So much of their married interaction had been overlain after all with the forever material bickering.

If nothing else, the so-called counseling with Preacher Brown, the subsequent encounter with Brown's wife Amy and then the lightening quick transformation of Preacher Brown's church into a mosque had had a galvanizing effect upon him vis-a-vis the Muslims. Thus in short order, he joined a frontier based group called *Americans for Americans* – which was surprisingly steeped in and bitterly opposed to *Islamic civilization jihad*. And he began to be active in social media posts – something he'd eschewed previously as being just one more symptom of the culture's shallowing.

Now though, he realized that it was every knowing citizen's responsibility to get the word out by any means possible; and, as intelligent as he was, his posts were biting and direct. So much so, that very soon, certain in government took serious notice as well.

Mora had questions – felt serious misgivings - seeing him devoting so much time now to the computer which he'd previously ignored. It was, of course, time she felt belonged to her and the children; then, on taking note of the content of his daily offerings, expressed more discomfort. 'Did he really think it was necessary or wise to wax so negative?' And, 'as residents of America, shouldn't Muslims be entitled to constitutional rights – to live and work and worship as *they* saw fit?'

"They have those rights as Americans," he responded, "but not if their dedicated objective is to overthrow the government."

Repercussions, however, were not particularly subtle. First, the IRS audited – though their combined incomes (Mona's from part time teaching and Jake's as a forestry technician) barely placed them above the poverty level. And yet, the government was very thorough, going back years and telephoning at all hours day and night for verifications. While all phone calls were apparently monitored as well – perhaps by the NSA – as strange *clickings* were periodically noticeable on the line.

Mona whined incessantly, repeatedly asking Jake why he couldn't devote half as much time to the care and feeding of *their* children. Then, when she discovered an article he'd left by the computer – a *Prophecy Today* piece on the Administration's secret plans for rounding up and incarcerating dissidents, she went completely *round the bend.*

"Look at this!" she screamed. "Is this what you're wanting for us? To get yourself locked in one of their camps with no one to take care of us at all?"

"No," he said, "I'm trying to publicize it so it won't happen to anyone!"

She left him then - packed up *her* children and retreated to her parents' place upstate. Nor was Jake home either when, several nights later, clandestine operatives in the best Stalinesque tradition came seeking under cover of darkness.

* * * *

High atop Pompey's Pillar, a towering rock formation alongside the Yellowstone River in south-central Montana, he sat very still, soaking up the silence while of course seeing none of the teeming buffalo, elk and wolves the great explorer William Clark had once reported down below. Clark had named the rock after Indian guide Sacajawea's young son – who he affectionately called *Little Pomp.* But then, of course that was a story that most moderns wouldn't know, or appreciate. Thomas Jefferson, the president then, and his predecessor the great John Adams were barely touched on now in schools, so why think that anyone would know or care about Lewis and Clark and their Corps of Discovery?

Not far from where he was sitting, also, was where (seventy years after William Clark) the famed Sioux Indian leader *Rain in the Face* had first drawn a bead on General George Armstrong Custer. Down below, Custer and his party were protecting an early railroad survey crew; and the fact that *Rain in the Face's* shot missed Custer and killed the Army's attending physician led to Custer's pursuit and eventual capture of the Indian. Interestingly, too – at least Jake Harwell found it interesting – several years later, after Rain in the Face had escaped from a military stockade, he was reported to have been the Sioux who fired the fatal shot that killed Custer at The Little Bighorn.

Jake Harwell stayed silent there for a long time, not wanting to leave the history and the feeling of the place – finally climbing down the Park Service scaffolding erected for modern folks and marveling at the fitness of Clark in 1804 and *Rain in the Face* later, who had scaled the vertical wall unaided.

The political left's line that the founding fathers were merely an out of touch bunch of patricians sitting around in long stockings and powdered wigs pontificating their way into liberty and the constitution had galled him – even before he fully understood the political rationale for such a stance. And the arguments for radical constitutional rejection or change – the monotonous plaint that changing times required changed laws denigrated the absolute genius of the truly gifted and adaptable framers. A mere cursory reading, for example, of the nuanced letters exchanged between John Adams and Thomas Jefferson and, for that matter, between John Adam's wife Abigail and Jefferson revealed intellect and learning light years *beyond* the grasp and knowledge of NOW – the 140 characters of the burgeoning "valley girl" mentality.

In fact, the contrast was so stark as to be breathtaking; and Harwell could only wish that the founder/patriots were present to apply their wisdom to NOW'S culturally rotted *sinking ship*.

Perhaps they would be so disquieted as to seek another *new world* somewhere else, though Harwell doubted it. It had been their mantra after all *never* to give up. But the ethos, for example, that aborting 60 million babies on the altar of convenience was somehow *civilized,* while ancient human sacrifices to the false god Moloch were *barbaric* certainly would challenge their logic. And taken together with politically correct gay marriage and transgenders wandering freely between *his* and *her* restrooms left Jake Harwell, deeply sensitive Christian that he was, wondering why judgment and sharia law hadn't come even sooner.

For the love of country – for the securing of her independence – John Adams had done impossible things. In Revolutionary times and before being the first Vice President and the second President, he was called away from the love of his life, wife Abigail, and family for YEARS. Braving towering North Atlantic seas on a sailing ship in midwinter and hiking a thousand miles over the snow clad Pyrenees to secure aid from the French; leader in the Continental Congress; chief advocate and signer of the Declaration of Independence; serious contributor to the Constitution; farmer; lawyer; first minister to London after the Revolutionary War; scholar; writer; husband; father; Christian; and avowed opponent to slavery. Who shared a symbol of God's approval of the Nation when he died on the same day as his friend and foe and friend again, the patriot Thomas Jefferson - on of all days, the Fourth of July.

'He was who we were; not what we've become!' Harwell thought. And angry, he scorned the NOW people for spitting on John Adam's grave. Not to mention upon the graves of the World War II veterans – who died at Normandy, Nijmegen and Anzio; and Okinawa, Iwo Jima and Tarawa – to defend the NOW people from the very fascist ideologies that they now embraced. Practicing, as a religion, political correctness - that powerful tool for *prevention* of dissent - while no doubt following soon enough with a labeling of the founders' expressed Christian values as unlawful and *hate speech* as well.

Desolate and directionless, Jake Harwell was alone with knowledge no longer welcomed, or even tolerated. Rejected, punished and scorned - thinking the only way he could show honor now was to not give up, as the framers never had. To go on surviving for as long as he could in the mountains they too had loved.

CHAPTER NINE

Women Stoned and Butchered in Saudi Arabia

"Saudi Arabia is the source of Islam and its quintessence. It is the place where the Muslim religion is practiced in its purest form, and it is the origin of much of the fundamentalist vision that has, in my lifetime, spread far beyond its borders. In Saudi Arabia, every breath, every step we took was infused with concepts of purity or sinning, and with fear. Wishful thinking about the peaceful tolerance of Islam cannot interpret away this reality: hands are still cut off; women still stoned and enslaved, just as the Prophet Mohammed decided centuries ago. . . . . When people say that the values of Islam are compassion, tolerance and freedom, I look at reality, at real cultures and governments, and I see that it simply is not so. People in the West swallow this sort of thing because they have learned not to examine the religions or cultures of minorities too critically for fear of being called racist."

–Ayaan Hirsi Ali, *Infidel*

"We who have known what it is to live without freedom watch with incredulity at you who call yourselves liberals — who claim to believe so fervently in individual liberty and minority rights —

make common cause with the forces in the world that manifestly pose the greatest threats to that very freedom and those very minorities."

–Ayaan Hirsi Ali, *Heretic*

When Amy Shiloh returned from Europe, she went directly to her parent's farm outside Indianapolis, glad to be back in America, glad for the safe feelings of familiarity. Her experience as a pastor's ex-wife didn't count for much in the labor market; but, since as a young girl, she had had much experience with horses and even excelled in various competitions, she soon was hired by a local stable. Then, she tended horses and gave riding lessons to children, distancing herself for a time from the troubling thoughts of Islam in Europe.

She had gone to a Bible College – not specifically to marry a pastor (as some girls do), but because of her strong faith and feelings from early on that she was meant to do things for her Lord. Then, as things worked out, she'd met Reverend Benjamin Brown at a school sponsored conference and so *had* married a pastor – something she now regretted every waking day. He'd been several years older and so seemingly self-assured that now, in retrospect, she couldn't understand how he'd turned out to be so weak. It was, she fretted, as if he'd reacted negatively to her own considerable strength, rather than feeding off of it. And in her continuing incomprehension, she resolved to one day query the Lord.

Her dad and mother, who were generally quiet, busy with the farm and much involved in their own church, expressed gladness that she was home, but did not press her immediately regarding her plans. Of course, they chatted some about great aunt Helena and Harald in Holland and at first Amy said nothing about the overriding threat of Islam. But then one day, when she made a passing reference in some conversation, her father returned that Muslims – the Muslim Student Association (MSA) had a farm now in not too distant Plainfield and also that Muslims were actively constructing mosques in

Indianapolis. At which point, Amy's short lived feelings of a return to safety were ended.

She opened up then as to what she'd learned in Europe, wondering more than before what the extent of it actually was in America. She expounded to her parents now on the Muslim visitations to Benjamin Brown's Fort Wayne church and her dark misgivings which Brown had ignored. Then, in spite of herself, she wondered increasingly what had happened to *their* church, led finally by curiosity to make the upstate drive. Rationalizing in part and telling herself it would be good *and Scriptural* to clear the air a bit, talk to Benjamin and pursue the course of forgiveness.

On reaching Fort Wayne, she got off at the familiar exit and turned down known streets. But then, on arriving at the church, discovered that there no longer was a church. Instead, there was a golden dome atop the familiar old building and a sign with Arabic lettering – which stated also in English, "Mid Central Mosque."

Thunderstruck, she pulled into the parking lot, sitting shocked for the moment, then thought finally to go inside and try at least to get word of Benjamin. However, as she got out of the car, unmistakable warning bells clanged in her head and stopped her in mid stride. Then, she saw them – a swarthy Arab man not far off at the corner, and another on the new mosque's front steps. And suddenly remembering Aunt Helena's dire warnings, she turned quickly back to the car, got in and sped away from the now predominantly Muslim neighborhood.

Badly shaken, she returned back South to her parents' farm, her mind a swirl of ideas. 'What had happened? And how? How had Benjamin's church transformed so rapidly into a mosque?' She *had* to know, of course - settling finally on trying to reach Benjamin through his parents.

She found their names and number in an old address book, thinking if Benjamin weren't at their home in Evansville, then at least they could tell her how to find him. However, she no sooner had identified herself than Benjamin's mother hung up the phone – Benjamin's fictions regarding her unfaithfulness having spread from son's church to parents' home.

So that then, Amy broke down; and afterwards her parents found her in her bedroom, weeping. She told them about Benjamin's *used to be* church, that was now a mosque, and about Benjamin's mother's rejection. But somehow, they couldn't go beyond to understand the deeper, darker forebodings she was feeling – in no small part because she couldn't totally explain them herself. When she spoke again of the Muslims, there was no exchange of knowing glances between her parents because, like nearly all American Christians, there was no real knowing. It was after all right out of the Muslim Brotherhood's playbook – that the American infidel would remain in the dark until it was too late.

Amy went to see her old instructor and mentor at the Bible College she'd attended in Indianapolis. Brother Anthony Kyle was thick set, gray haired and bushy browed, with black eyes that commanded respect. And inevitably, he was referred to as "God" by silly undergraduates, never out of malice, but more with genuine awe.

Brother Kyle seemed always to have the right answers, whatever the subject, as his *no holds barred* logic seemed to cut to the very heart of all matters. He had been Amy's academic advisor and, what with her quick intelligence, she had been undoubtedly one of his favorites – though certainly such preference was never uttered.

Slender, blond, with troubled gray eyes and no makeup, she showed up unannounced at his office door and, five years after having seen her last, recognition was nevertheless immediate.

"Amy!" he said, rising from his desk. "Come in, for heaven sakes! Come in!"'

In tan outdoorsman's vest and dark work pants, he led her by the hand into his small, book-lined study - which like Kyle himself was not in the least bit fancy. Then, offering her a chair alongside the cluttered desk and sensing she was distressed and not there for a mere social call, he crossed back to close the door.

After which, she told him – unloaded on him – all of it, with intensity, tears and even occasional elicited smiles, exhibiting the full range of a talented and sensitive young woman's feelings. And Brother Kyle listened intently, seated on a chair alongside, his dark eyes mirroring the deep caring that had made him a legend. Head cocked to the side and offering only an occasional quiet prompting.

He was not judgmental regarding the divorce. In fact, he said nothing about it, never indicating at all what he remembered or thought about Benjamin Brown, and only volunteering to find out what he could about his whereabouts.

However, Amy's rant about the Muslims was a different matter; and, in that her concern was matched by his own, he became by degrees more animated, first nodding his head at her assertions, then in the end taking the lead.

"Amy," he said, his deep grave tone less than reassuring, "unfortunately, you're right and you've figured it out. And for sure it's a serious enough threat that people shouldn't have to be stumbling over it before being informed. One might legitimately ask, too, 'where has our vaunted investigative media been – if not downright complicit?' They are supposed to be the eyes and ears of a free people. But then, that begs the question where has the clergy been as well? – we who are supposed to be most in tune with spiritual dangers.

"Through Title VI, our government has essentially encouraged Saudi Arabia to write our schools' curriculum – if you can even imagine that! So that from K through 12, we've got American children studying the five pillars of Islam, while the mention of anything Christian or Jewish is prohibited. Kids unknowingly are learning *the acceptance of Islam prayer* which is an invitation to the demonic.

"And then there are our Bible Colleges! And how terribly we've failed, as evidenced by our sending out ill-prepared young pastors like Benjamin Brown, who seemingly was a sheep led to a slaughter. Amy, I'm just so sorry!"

He sat with his head bowed for a moment and, reflexively, she reached over to touch his hand.

" Brother Kyle, what can I do?" she said, "I feel like such a coward for not going in the church – the mosque – in Fort Wayne, at least to find out what happened!"

"No!" he said, snapping back to attention. "You were exactly right to do what you did. Something bad could have happened – probably would have happened. You see, now because of political correctness, Muslims are not held accountable. Increasingly, they can do pretty much anything they want in their own neighborhoods and nobody says boo."

Once again, Amy was leaning forward, listening and remembering what she'd learned in Europe.

"Furthermore," Brother Kyle continued, "according to them, there have to be limits on our own freedom of speech – limits about which they insist it's time to debate. For example, they say if (according to them) we've insulted Allah, then of necessity we must pay a penalty, possibly with our lives. Which ultimately means, in their curiously weighted system of logic, that since freedom of speech represents an incitement to blasphemy, it's probably not worth having at all. And they, of course, are the only ones free to determine what blasphemy is. Nevertheless, it's something which our multi-cultural elitist crowd are seriously considering. People who can't even seem to get their arms around the simplistic notion that *tolerance for intolerance is not tolerance at all.*

"You know, after our immigration policy was changed in the late 1960's, they began pouring in from a whole host of countries – from the former Palestine and Egypt and Yemen and Pakistan; from Saudi Arabia (which has contributed virtually tens of billions of oil money dollars to the building of mosques); from Afghanistan and Turkey and Iran (with its *Shia* slant); and Albania (which provided the Muslim Mafia); and also from Somalia, whose resistance to assimilation was and is the most noteworthy for their continuing practice of female genital mutilation."

He paused at her involuntary gasp.

"They do that here, too?" she managed weakly.

"Oh yeah," he said grimly. "And honor killings. Everything!

"Look," he said, "they came here with a plan and now, fifty years later, we are just becoming vaguely aware of this Trojan horse in our midst. In part, it can be summarized in the Muslim Brotherhood's anti-assimilation motto which goes something like: 'We are Muslims first and last and forever. And we should live only as Muslims and die as Muslims.' And further, in outlining their plan for grand jihad and the elimination and destruction of western civilization, they set up a strategy of what we might call *reverse assimilation* – that is a steady process in which Muslim immigrants and converts gradually impose their values and ultimately their *sharia* law on complacent Americans."

Again he paused momentarily, allowing the stricken Amy to catch her breath.

"It sounds like what happened in Europe," she said finally, weakly.

"Precisely," he said, "and for the West in general it's projected to all come tumbling down. The Muslim Brotherhood, which this President has so warmly embraced, has over 100 million members worldwide devoted to the ideal of Islamization – which is that it's the duty of every Muslim to strive towards making all peoples Muslim. Towards that end, they have been responsible for the creation of *Hamas*, which of course is dedicated to the destruction of Israel; have assisted in the creation of *Al-Qaeda*, as a base for their holy war against the West; and can boast of a whole pantheon of infamous terrorist members as well.

"They've been allowed to operate here in the States through the Muslim Student Association (MSA), which in fact was the first Islamic organization to be established nationally. And they have centers right here in Indiana – including the Islamic Teaching Center in Indianapolis for the indoctrination of Arab youth and also African Americans in prisons. Besides which, they've purchased a farm in Plainfield, which I believe is actually a center for many of their finance management activities."

"I've heard something about the farm," Amy put in, as he paused, grateful at least to know something – anything – about what he was so thoroughly detailing. "But of course, I just thought it was a farm."

He snorted. "I'm sure they collect government farm subsidies every year all right, but believe me there aren't any significant crops being produced.

"Oh, Amy," he said grimly. "I've just scratched the surface. The Muslim Brotherhood is linked to at least two thousand nonprofit organizations – at least some of which have been prosecuted for aiding and abetting worldwide terrorists, and all of which are targeting our ultimate destruction. Besides which, there are Muslim Student Associations located on six hundred college and university campuses; hundreds of Islamic Societies; and hundreds of chapters of the Muslim American Society, the Council of American Islamic Relations (known as CAIR) and all kinds of others."

"Brother Kyle, it's as if we're fifty years behind," she managed weakly, as he paused. "Is there any hope of stopping them?"

For a moment, he looked at her – studying her.

"Amy, I don't know," he said. "Under our Constitution, they have the right to exist."

"Agreed," she said, "but given the blueprint you've described, how is it possible for us to co-exist?"

"I don't know, Amy," he said again. "But we do know that we have Christ and, as theirs is an aggressive and demonic rooted religion attacking us, we have to resist - while still offering their unsaved members, as much as possible, the right path, the only path, and regardless the consequences.

"Amy, as late in the day as it is, some of us are seriously organizing. And if you want to join with us, I'll vouch for you and I know you'll be welcomed. And I believe we'll be able to find a job for you here on campus – to at least put food on your table."

"Brother Kyle," she responded, surprised by the tears welling up in her eyes, "I want to help, you know that! But, I'm just not understanding why it's come to this. Why, if you knew all this, weren't you and others organizing sooner, and at least letting the rest of us know?"

"Amy," he said wearily, "that's the worst part of all. We didn't know. They've been clever in hiding their true objectives – right in the open as it were. And we've been so smug and self-satisfied. 'Oh, this is America, and it could never happen here!' Amy, what I've told you today, I've only learned myself in the past year. Which puts us, not fifty years behind as you.

CHAPTER TEN

The Compromising Church

. . . With the accelerated pace of the attack on religious liberty today, there could develop a great divide in the church between confessing churches and compromising churches similar to what happened in Nazi Germany.

"This will not be a divide based on denominational affiliation but based on the degree of loyalty to biblical fidelity. It is sad but true that more and more believers will be compromising core biblical values and standards rather than be stigmatized or persecuted, and lose influence in society....

"The confessing church is penalized by the state government. The compromising church is applauded by the state government. While the confessing church is hunted down and ostracized by the humanistic state, the compromising church is celebrated by the far left radicals and used as a model of how church and state should function together....

"The confessing church desires the praise of God. The compromising church desires the praise of men. Ultimately at the end of the day it boils down to this: Are we living for the praise of men or the praise of God? If things don't change in the coming days, we will be shocked at how many mega-churches, mid-size churches and smaller churches compromise the word of God so they can continue to keep their doors open.

–Joseph G. Mattera,
"8 Clear Signs of A Compromising Church"
Prophecy News Watch – December 3, 2014

Eloise Turner, accomplished black woman and Guy Alexander's former fiancé was much troubled by Guy's last comment to her regarding the Islamization of America. Having seen firsthand what had happened to the France that she had loved, she realized full well that such a fate at home was not impossible. And, while like most African Americans, she had serious issues with the country's past, still she very much regarded America as *her* country and was intensely proud of the corrective steps which had been taken. They were steps which had contributed mightily to her receiving an outstanding education and a so-called "seat at the table." And if acknowledging that made her a *sell out* or *Uncle Tom* in the eyes of some blacks, she thought, 'well so be it!'

Eloise Turner was anything but weak. However, now she went looking for a church. Raised Christian in deep South Mississippi, she'd been away with her family in France in her teenage years. There, because of imperfect mastery of the French language, their church going had lapsed. Then later, back in the States when she'd gone up North to elitist college, religion hadn't been *cool* at all and she'd fallen away completely.

Now however, with a woman's dark horror at Islam's looming *sharia*, a tiny flame was re-ignited. In a passing conversation with colleagues, the name of Jesus had been mentioned in some context or other; at which she'd felt unexpected and surprising feelings of peace and assurance wash over her. It was fleeting, but palpable all the same. And still curious later on in her apartment, she'd pulled out an old Bible and felt the peacefulness again.

She hunted hard for a church over the next six weeks, sampling a different one from the long list each Sunday, and even attending others on Wednesday nights. And generally speaking, the people were nice and friendly and some of the music was uplifting. However, a preached word regarding the Muslim threat was not to be found, let alone any answers or directions as to what might be done about it. She even interviewed (unofficially) several preachers afterwards and uniformly, in answer to the question what they thought of the coming Islamization, they returned blank looks or, in one case, a politically correct, "no comment!"

More troubled than ever, and now with a tinge of disgust, she went online, searching out various other churches in the D.C. area, reading painstakingly through their stated manifestos. Still, she found almost nothing regarding the burning issues of the day and stands against, for example, homosexuality, gay marriage and abortion – let alone any mention of demonic Islam. Churches wanting to be all things to all people, or - as she thought cynically – 'willing to accept contributions from all people equally.'

However then, when she was about ready to give up, she hit on one in Alexandria whose words struck with immediate force. It was a little church with the name of *Resurrection Chapel*. And the text boldly proclaimed the absolute uncompromising truth of God's word.

"If you are Muslim, homosexual, a married gay, or someone who thinks it's all right to practice abortion or discrimination during the week and then come here on Sundays with a plastic Jesus smile, forget about it! Come here wanting and expecting to change, or don't come at all. We don't co-exist with any of the above. We are followers of Jesus Christ; we love you and will show you the right path. But while Christ loves you as well, He doesn't countenance any of the above practices either."

Eloise was struck with inclusion of the word *Muslim* on the list, and especially at the top. So that in spite of the church's relative distant whereabouts, she went there – soon learning that the *Muslim* was indeed so positioned as to attract fearless recruits like the one she soon would become.

Resurrection Chapel was non-denominational and under the leadership of a brave young black pastor, Douglas Bowles, who was developing an outreach to other area churches – dedicated in fact to the education of other pastors as to the looming danger of Islamic jihad. Pastor Bowles was endeavoring to do this through personal visitations by himself and his staff, along with the planned publication and dissemination of various pamphlets outlining the Muslim stealth attack.

After only a couple of visits, Eloise volunteered to help with the publishing, knowing that, as a Congressional staffer, she could access information not generally made available. And after an extensive and probative interrogation by Pastor Bowles, she was accepted – then admonished that what they were doing was not for the faint of heart, and that he, Pastor Bowles, fully expected at some point that the chapel would be bombed.

"This business about Islam being a peaceful religion is so much hooey," he said. "The ones that are peaceful are simply invested in the jihad in other ways, and so you'll never see them rising up in strong and sincere criticism of the violence. They are fighting an overall jihad in the name of Allah in order to impose *sharia* on the world; and so you can't say that Al-Qaeda or ISIS, or any of them, are perverting Islam. They are the military arm and are advancing it. And ultimately, you can expect the Muslims here in America to use whatever means – violent or otherwise – to reach their goals."

At work in the Congressional Office Building, Eloise used her lunch hours and additional free time to research Islamization and was astonished at the amount of information not in general circulation – information, she supposed, not deemed noteworthy enough for release, or general consumption. And while reasons for release or non-release seemed nebulous at best, she hadn't worried herself with such questions previously at all.

Rather, as the insatiable policy wonk that she was, she had devoured reams of information all right, reading endlessly to understand the minutia of government. But then, like most everybody else, had just ignored Islamic news, viewing everything about it as basically inconsequential.

Now however, given her recent experiences in Europe, everything clicked into place, and she was ever more alarmed. Not too long after her re-commitment at *Resurrection Chapel*, in fact, she came across a publication written by Dr. Mohamed Akram Adlouni (one of the architects of the Muslim Brotherhood) that put the jihad in America into much clearer focus. Among other things, it stated that the *conquest* of the United States would not happen overnight, but that ultimately Muslims 'would have devout believers in positions of power; operate their own television networks; publish their own newspapers; affect the curriculum in public schools and colleges; establish Islamic universities to train Islamic scholars; set up an Islamic Central Bank to extend free loans to all believers; and of course a Central Islamic Court to establish *sharia* law throughout the land.'

And noting that the paper was published in 1991, Eloise grimly ticked off in her mind those things which had already happened fully, or at least in part.

Then she read on – 'that all idolatry would be restricted; that women would be obliged to dress moderately and to obey the commands of their husbands; girls would be forbidden to visit doctors or hospitals without a male relative; homosexuality and pornography would be outlawed; the sale of alcohol prohibited; musical instruments of all types banned; movie theaters shut down; television programs heavily censored; Jews and Christians required to wear defined distinctive dress; all non-Muslims to pay a poll tax; fornicators fined and imprisoned; adulterers stoned; thieves with their hands cut off; and apostasy resulting in decapitation or crucifixion.'

This Muslim Brotherhood *success in America*, the article concluded, 'would be the first step in the establishment of the global Islamic state.'

Eloise was alone in the office at night, after work, reading; and this particular article struck a chord with her as none other. So that, she was chilled and frightened to the point of stopping herself with an effort from calling Pastor Bowles right then and there. Only his warning 'that they keep their conversations to a minimum' prevented her, agreeing with him as she did about the dangers of the new age of surveillance.

"Look," he'd said, "I don't know who's watching or listening to us, if anyone. But there's no point in accelerating our notoriety."

At any rate, though, the reading of such documents soon gave Eloise new perspectives on various American leaders' and their cluelessness as well. After the 9/11 attacks, for example, President George W. Bush had enlisted Imam Muzzammil H. Siddiqi, the president of the Islamic Society of North America to represent the Muslim community and say a prayer for the victims in the National Cathedral. Just the year before, Siddiqi had strongly criticized the U.S. for its support of Israel, saying, "If you remain on the side of injustice, the wrath of God will come." While in other messages, he had endorsed violent jihad and stood firm against Muslims serving in the U.S. military. Nevertheless, Eloise recalled that Bush had lauded him after the Cathedral prayer, saying he'd done a "heck of a job" and how proud the country was to have had him there.

Furthermore, that was not the only time that George Bush appeared to be completely out of touch with Muslim reality. In fact, he made Sheikh Hamza Yusuf the White House Advisor on Muslim Affairs in the months after 9/11 - who then became one of the more frequent visitors to the oval office despite his past statements that he did not believe in the false gods of American society 'whether they were known as Jesus, or democracy, or the bill of rights.'

Then, too, there was the even more stunning revelation that after providing Muslim support in Bush's re-election bid in 2000, Abdurahman M. Alamoudi and his software and security firm, Ptech, Inc., were awarded lucrative contracts with several government agencies, including the United States Armed Forces, NATO, the Department of Energy, the Department of Justice, the FBI, the FAA, the IRS, the Secret Service *and* the White House. And even after the Ptech office in Boston was raided in 2002, amid allegations that the firm was funding international terrorism, the company had continued to obtain government contracts and to operate with top level military clearance.

Other bizarre examples stood out, as well, at almost every level of the government. But immediately, Eloise focused more on the current U.S. president – his Muslim roots and thinly veiled endorsements of the Muslim Brotherhood, both at home and abroad. And she wondered, and notwithstanding his denials, if his true identity would not prove to be the culmination of the fifty year Islamic deception.

Thinking! Thinking! She was beside herself, often wondering if the Islamist hadn't already won. Certainly they believed they had, she thought. And amazingly, due to the continuing genius of the Muslim Brotherhood's hiding jihad under the protective umbrella of political correctness, twelve years after 9/11, there was more than ever a reluctance to even name the enemy. The President himself, for example, wouldn't so much as utter the phrase *Islamic terrorists.*

Eloise chafed at the idea that the Muslim Brotherhood had had for many years strategic and operational plans in place and were, after all those years of Americans sleeping, well organized, funded and disciplined. And she struggled, trying to convey the huge, almost incomprehensible danger in the little pamphlets she'd volunteered to write for Pastor Bowles. There was so much information but, with the clock ticking, the challenge was to be *immediately* impactful. With The Brotherhood having thousands of nonprofit organizations nationwide, working *daily* to overthrow the government and ultimately obliterate the founding principles, she thought despairingly that it really might be too late.

CHAPTER ELEVEN

Where Will The Martyrs Come From?

At some point we will have to stand the ultimate test, which is whether we desire God more than we love our lives, or whether we love our pleasures, conveniences and material goods more than God. Truly, if we confess Christ before men He will confess us before His Father in heaven, but if we deny Him before men He will deny us before His Father in heaven."

–Joseph G. Mattera,
"8 Clear Signs of a Compromising Church"
Prophecy News Watch – December 3, 2014

Pastor Douglas Bowles was a black man in his mid- thirties, gone prematurely gray. The burning fire in his eyes that made them look at times almost red testified of an intense spirit seemingly ready to jump right out of his skin.

"Pat," he would say over and over to his tall, slender and equally black wife, "there's no time, Pat! There's no time!"

To which she would respond calmly, quietly, patiently – continuing on with whatever she was doing. Understanding in her quiet spirit the balance she provided – the balance which he had to have.

Like Eloise, both Douglas and Pat had roots in Mississippi, their next door neighbor parents having migrated together north to the Capitol at the height of Jim Crow. There, Douglas' father had become in fact a Capitol police officer – a black officer with a driving work ethic, which in turn was reflected in a scornful attitude towards those who didn't try.

Douglas had inherited that drive, had been not only an honor student but an athlete – declining several scholarship offers nevertheless and knowing from early on he was to serve the Lord. He was still in Bible College in fact when he first tried to marry Patricia – whom he'd known forever. She, however, was on her own path, studying to be a doctor and rejecting his petitions until after she'd finished med school several years later. Then afterwards, they'd struggled together through her internships and his assistant pastorates, somehow and with the help of parents raising two children along the way.

"No wonder, you're prematurely gray," Patricia would chide him.

To which he'd reply, "The wonder is that you're *not!*"

They both loved Eloise from the beginning, took her into their home and shared confidences. No doubt, it was in part because of their shared Mississippi roots, but also, there was in all three of them an unwavering commitment to excellence which contributed to the rapport.

Patricia confided that she – like Eloise – was viewed by many blacks as having *strayed from the plantation*, as being an *Uncle Tom* for essentially turning from her poor black roots to pursue success in the white man's world.

"It makes me sick," she said. "God's way is to maximize the talents He's given us, and to use them on the pathways He directs. And in my life, I've dealt with all manner of people along those paths, you name it, blacks, whites, brown, yellow, rich, poor, whatever. And very few seemed ever to care about the color of the doctor's skin, as long as they were ultimately made well."

Douglas sounded angrier. "Instead of getting off their backsides and making something of themselves," he raged, "our black brothers and sisters prefer to play the victim. It's far easier to have a pity party, than to work a job; and, of course, the hated white man's government will always take care – with food stamps, or unemployment insurance, or a myriad of other giveaway programs, the very existence of which prove in their pathetic minds that they really must be victims and really are owed. Never wanting to explain and studiously ignoring, in fact, the parallel track programs designed for their free or cheap education, and the legitimate escape from the poverty they're so often whining about."

They were sitting out on the screened in sun porch in the pastor's home, sipping cool lemonade against the late afternoon heat of summer – Douglas, Patricia and Eloise.

"So," the Pastor said, "to show how black they are, how rebellious they can be vis-a-vis the white man, they have now cut off their noses despite their face – casting away Jesus as *the white man's God* and embracing the truly laughable (at least at first) Nation of Islam sham – the black American version of a traveling medicine show. Which now, with the huge influx of true Islamists from the Middle East and elsewhere, has been blended into something with serious dogma – something horrific and demonic!"

Eloise sat silent, listening. Usually, because of her superior intellect, she found herself more in a teaching or mentoring position of her own. But now, she was absorbing, though not at all enjoying what she was taking in.

Douglas Bowles first ran afoul of the Muslims, he said, on a prison visit. He'd gone to a particular prison – a high security facility – for the first time, as a former parishioner sentenced there had written him a moving letter.

Dear Pastor Bowles: I'm a dead man in here if I don't agree to convert to Islam. I know I don't merit any sympathy, and I'm not asking for any. I'm locked up deservedly, but that shouldn't deprive me of my core belief in Christ. Pastor, can you please come, so that we might at least pray?

—Neil Stormer

Pastor Bowles went. Then he was blindsided with the discovery of a whole new evolving, Muslim orchestrated world of imprisonment. In fact, he found out later it had originated at a prison in New York – Greenhaven Federal Prison – and was metastasizing across the entire country, as Muslim demands were being met with spineless political correctness and capitulation. So that the result was a new thriving Muslim prison agenda, in effect a system within the system.

In the brief visit, Neil Stormer explained it as best he could – a small, tortured white man, balding, shaking and obviously very much afraid. He was a man with a wife and three small children on the outside, imprisoned on a convoluted embezzling case for which he'd actually received no money and never himself quite understood.

"Just the fact that you're visiting me in here, Pastor, may make you a target, too," he said – a heartfelt statement Bowles received initially as just paranoiac.

"They don't much tolerate Christians in here," Stormer said, "and the two chaplains we have right now are both Muslims. If a new guy comes in and wants to convert, he's protected. But otherwise, he's fair game for everybody – blacks, Hispanic street gangsters, white supremacists – you name it!"

Pastor Bowles prayed with him, but only ritualistically Bowles came to believe later on – praying Jesus would keep him strong, while still not really understanding. Then afterwards, troubled in his spirit, and by the fact of being spit upon and yelled at by several Muslims on his way out, he was driven to do his own research. Which led finally to incredulity as he learned in fact that in many prison locations Muslims were being given the right to establish their own mosques with their own chosen imams; their own separate kitchens serving *halal* meals; and separate hours for showers and toilet. Furthermore, because of their claims of Islamic code violations, they were declared free from strip searches and frisking.

So that in fact, they were established as a privileged class in which, as Neil Stormer had stated, membership was desirable if for no other reason than the protection it afforded. Which ultimately translated into the fact, too, that the Islamists had successfully established one more powerful evangelizing forum.

Neil Stormer had continued to resist, though, and was ultimately murdered not too long after their meeting – which was one of the things which drove Bowles daily.

"Of course," he said, "the Saudis – those great benefactors – took note of the resulting rising rate of prison conversions; then promptly poured in additional millions to fund what's called the National Association of Muslim Chaplains. And, who can compete with that? Millions! I'm saying millions!"

Eloise walked with Douglas and Patricia on a wooded path behind the Bowles' home – idyllic and far removed for a time from their conversations. So much so, that one might believe the *Muslim march* was just a dark nightmare that didn't actually exist. This was the general perception, Eloise knew – that things were all right and, because this was America, they would always be all right. Which was, of course, the basis for the Islamic stealth attack – that life went on as normal with hardly anyone noticing.

Pastor Bowles held his wife Patricia's hand and, as they all three paused beside a small trickling stream, it was a time of quiet loving and friendship. At least to the casual observer, it would seem as such – a black man loving his wife and the two walking with a friend in peaceful surroundings. But, as the three paused by the bubbling water, the pastor's prayer was in fact about the soon enveloping darkness – which only they could see.

CHAPTER TWELVE

Government Surveillance
of Americans

The National Security Agency has a secret backdoor into its vast databases under a legal authority enabling it to search for US citizens' email and phone calls without a warrant, according to a top-secret document passed to the Guardian by Edward Snowden.

The previously undisclosed rule change allows NSA operatives to hunt for individual Americans' communications using their name or other identifying information. Senator Ron Wyden told the Guardian that the law provides the NSA with a loophole potentially allowing "warrantless searches for the phone calls or emails of law-abiding Americans".

The authority, approved in 2011, appears to contrast with repeated assurances from Barack Obama and senior intelligence officials to both Congress and the American public that the privacy of US citizens is protected from the NSA's dragnet surveillance programs.

The intelligence xdata is being gathered under Section 702 of the of the Fisa Amendments Act (FAA), which gives the NSA authority to target without warrant the communications of foreign targets, who must be non-US citizens and outside the US at the point of collection.

The communications of Americans in direct contact with foreign targets can also be collected without a warrant, and the intelligence agencies acknowledge that purely domestic communications can also be inadvertently swept into its databases. That process is known as "incidental collection" in surveillance parlance.

But this is the first evidence that the NSA has permission to search those databases for specific US individuals' communications. . . . .

–"NSA Loophole Allows Warrantless
Search for US Citizens' Emails and Phone Calls"
The Guardian Newspaper
August 9, 2013

Fifty years after the Muslim Brotherhood began their civilization jihad in America, forty-eight Christian resisters held a secret first meeting in St. Louis. It was a destination accessible to many by car and thus privacy protective - the caution testament to how far Islam had progressed in the assault on free speech.

Realizing the lateness of the hour, the men and women stood strong in their faith, with the template of Joshua in the forefront and their knowledge of the Lord's ability to do much with very little. They came from various parts of the country – people with interconnected ties of trust evolved over a generation of mutual service to the Lord. And among them were Brother Kyle from Amy Shiloh's Bible College in Indianapolis and Pastor Bowles from Eloise Turner's *Resurrection Chapel* in Virginia – men who had never met previously, but knew of one another by reputation.

Unlike many gatherings of God's people, this one was somber from the start. Prayer was penitent; praise and worship muted; and seriousness near to smothering. The United States of America – in many respects a lighthouse to the world – was on the verge of becoming a Muslim nation with *sharia* law; and those present felt a desperate weight of responsibility, in part because of their own neglect.

"Oh God help us!" was the theme. And "oh God show us what to do!" was the prayer. They prayed and thought; and broke up in small groups to pray some more and talk. Then brought back ideas for general discussion. And while there was some encouragement in the sharing, there remained the grim realization that, without the Lord's direct intervention, it was probably too late.

Still, they formulated various courses of action, somewhat tailored to fit the different regions and populations. Aware now of the true nature of jihad – that violence was an acceptable *when necessary* tool – they realized that most probably all those participating in the end would be martyred.

Reaching other pastors and congregations was critical, as there were many thousands of churches across the landscape still in darkness. And while doubtless some of their leaders understood the signs, many were muzzled by fear and feelings of isolation. Also, though national media could not be counted upon in any way, it was agreed that local papers and stations might be convinced to reveal Muslim Brotherhood front groups and their stealth agendas.

The ugly reality that Islam was a demonic driven cult and not the "peaceful religion" so widely portrayed weighed heavily on the conference, though. And the grim truth that many seminaries had downgraded the demonic, even placing it like miracles and healing in the dustbin of history, had resulted in a generation of clergy unable to function fully or explain. In many cases, a *re-education* was probably called for; but, with the clock ticking, there didn't seem to be enough time.

The subtle ways of the *Enemy* were noted – for example, the *apparent* behind the scenes Islamic funding of the homosexual lobby, which ran counter to their stern public opposition. The ultimate goal being that the homosexuals would so succeed with their sickening minority agenda that the vast majority of the population finally would be offended to the point of welcoming solutions of *sharia law*.

Questions of how best to disseminate the truth were discussed throughout - with consideration given to sufficient funding and efficient use of whatever Christian media might be available. And also the publication of information tracks and the need for brave foot soldiers to distribute them with fervor to groups of hundreds or even thousands, as it was well past time for one on one enlightenments.

* * * *

Afterwards, within ninety days of the leaders' meeting in St. Louis, in fact, Amy Shiloh was an organizer at a massive Christian women's rally in Washington D.C. Nearly a quarter of a million women were marching up Pennsylvania Avenue, singing hymns and waving placards, sick to death of their depiction by the secular media and the White House as being – for the unforgiveable sin of staying home with their children – unsophisticated *breeding sows*. And while the charge might be levelled that they'd been somewhat misdirected into attending, nevertheless, thanks to Resurrection Chapel's distributed packets, they finally were made aware also of the Islamic threat.

In fact, the dispensed knowledge had added an immediate extra edge which Guy Alexander, longtime reporter of DC demonstrations, sensed rather quickly. Standing on the sidewalk in front of a favorite bistro several blocks from the White House, he took note of a tall, slender blond woman who was at the moment not marching with the others, but in fact communicating via walkie-talkie with someone in the rear.

He approached and, as she finished her transmission, introduced himself as a member of the press, displaying his badge. To which she responded with a shrug.

"So?" she said coldly – certainly not in the friendly Christian manner he might have expected.

"I'm sorry," he said, "I wonder if I might just ask you a couple of questions?"

"Why, so you can use whatever I say to advance the narrative that we're fools?"

"No, no! Nothing like that! I'm just curious about the crowd – the huge turnout. And I think our readers would like to know what's driving it. You do want others to know, right?"

She looked at him more closely then – examiningly – a tall, slender black man, handsome in a gray windbreaker and jaunty gray Scottish cap.

"Look," he said, "I have no axe to grind. Just doin' my job and gettin' a story."

"You may not have an axe to grind, but whoever's pulling your strings probably does."

"Meaning?"

"Meaning, who has the last word on what stays in your story and how it's finally slanted."

"Look," he said solicitously, "instead of standing here jousting, how about if we just sit down for a cup of coffee? We can sit right out here at one of the tables on the sidewalk, and that way you won't be missing anything."

And afterwards, she wasn't sure why she'd agreed, though part of it she knew was just the opportunity for *her* to interview one of *them*.

"Are you sure you're not just hitting on a white woman?" she asked as soon as they were seated, further disarming him. "I've heard you black guys regard us as trophies."

And again he stared at her, the journalist in him trying to understand what in the world was driving the thinly veiled antagonism. As a member of the elitist media, he was used after all to a certain deference.

"Look, let's get this out of the way right up front, he said, "I'm gay!" – not quite believing it himself, and in fact much conflicted by his seeming ambiguity – often rationalizing his lapses as coming only when he was very drunk.

"Oh, I never would have guessed!" she said.

"Well, you Christians don't believe anybody's gay, right?" he said.

"We believe people stray, or are misled."

"Oh, and that's just a load!" he returned, leaning forward with lowered voice belying his intensity.

"I think deep down you know it's not," she said. "And besides, what makes you so sure your opinion is more valid than ours?"

"Science!" he snapped, "science!"   Still more than a little impressed by her lack of intimidation.

"Pooh, science!" she sniffed. "Science by whom?"

"By anybody that's anybody!" he returned. "But listen, I thought Christians were supposed to be *gentle as doves.* Not full on angry like yourself!"

"Oh, so now you know Scripture, Mister Gay Man?" she said with the slightest hint of a twinkle.

"Damn!" he said.

"So, if you're not really gay, but just experimenting, you really are hitting on me, eh?"

"Look, just let me ask you about the issues at hand," he said, suddenly defensive, "and that'll be it. What is it that you people want? I see the placards in the parade for *fairness in the media,* but what exactly is it that you would deem fair?"

"Now that I've got you here," she said, ignoring his question, "why is it that you folks have never reported on the Islamization of our country, and have spent so much of your resources tearing down Christianity which offers the best defense, if not the only defense, against *sharia?* Are you knowing or unknowing dupes for the Muslims? That's my question!"

His mouth dropped open – staggered by her assault.

"Here's a news flash for you!" she went on. "A real news flash! ISIS and Al-Qaeda are not perverting *sharia.* They're simply fulfilling it as warrior arms of the total system. And no again! Islam is not a peaceful religion! The ones not doing the violence are making no moves to stop it; so, they're complicit. And the Muslim Brotherhood has said as much – 'that they are all Muslims fighting jihad in the name of Allah.' So, why don't you believe them? Do you really think if you don't say it, they'll just soften up and go away?"

Actually coming partially undone, he spoke softly then, so that she could barely hear. "I've tried to say it," he said. "I wrote about it and they pulled my story. And I still don't know why."

Which made it her turn to stare – an interlude broken by a static blast from the handheld.

"Amy!" s male voice called.

"Yes!"

"The last of them are ready to leave."

"Okay, that's fine," she returned, looking out at the street. "Everything's still flowing smoothly here."

"What? What was that? Didn't copy that!"

"Good! Everything's good!"

"Okay! Roger that!"

She set the radio back down on the table.

"You liberals," she said, still angry, "you portray yourselves as the great protectors of women, only to be de facto supporters of *sharia*. Even you must understand that that makes no sense!"

"Look Amy," he said, taking a deep breath. "Now at least I know your first name - if not your last, or where you come from, or anything else. But I really wish we could continue this conversation later on. Would you consider giving me your name and number?"

"Oh right!" she said, "so you could sick the NSA on me, or some other government watch dog. I don't think so!"

"Well, they're more apt to be watching me than you at this point," he said, "but I understand what you're saying. If you should ever want to get in touch though, I'd deeply appreciate it."

Standing, he handed her his card, then turned and walked away, not catching her eyes' fleeting regret.

CHAPTER THIRTEEN

Leader's Sad End

In the Northwest corner of North Dakota where the two great rivers, Yellowstone and Missouri, meet and where Lewis and Clark rendezvoused on their way home in 1806, the Army built a huge compound called Fort Buford. It served as an offloading supply depot for many of their western operations; and Sitting Bull, the great Sioux chief hated it because many of the unloaded supplies were used in campaigns against his people. Thus, he organized many raids on the fort, so that soldiers stationed there rarely felt safe enough to stray far from their barracks. And once while walking through the post's ancient graveyard, Jake Harwell had taken note of the many headstones marked only with the words, "Died of Indian Attack."

After defeating Custer at the Little Bighorn, and pursued by avenging soldiers, Sitting Bull had led his band into Canada. They stayed there for some four years, but it was a sparse existence and finally, without food, they returned to the same Fort Buford to surrender. Which took place inside a small, still standing clapboard building - maintained until recently by the Park Service.

Barely surviving himself, Jake Harwell reached the Fort again in the late fall. The building was locked up; all the signs and historic markers had been done away with; and park service personnel were also long gone. A chill wind blew and *scattered forlorn, yellowing leaves as he leaned his head tiredly against the old building, trying as before to visualize where the Sioux band might have dismounted. He thought of Sitting Bull, perhaps his greatest American hero - who people no longer knew about at all – comparing the desolation he felt in his own life now and on his return."*

Back in his apartment in the evening, Guy Alexander reviewed the events of the day, thinking in particular about the young woman Amy and what she'd said. In fact, he remained surprised at the discomfort she'd engendered in him on several levels, while admitting to himself at the same time just how much he'd liked her.

He examined one of the pamphlets her group had made available to the marchers – one he'd found dropped in the street – surprised by the content and impressed by the writing and skilled condensation of women's enslavement under *sharia*. It depicted the experience of a young Muslim woman, whose charge of rape lacked the absurd but obligatory eye witness testimony of four male witnesses – so that in fact the girl herself was stoned to death. And he thought this, and other examples, shined a definitive light of warning for the 'long time kept in the dark' assembled marchers.

Still, on reaching the end of the tract, Guy Alexander was brought up short by the small print at the bottom which petitioned for funds and included the name and address of the tract's producer: *Resurrection Chapel of Alexandria*. And he groaned, instinctively recognizing a serious strategic blunder. It was after all a veritable invitation to violence when targeting a group as volatile as the Muslims - who could interpret a sneeze as an affront to the prophet. Sighing, he put the leaflet aside then, unaware that most of the writing he'd admired had been the handiwork of his former fiancée, Eloise Turner, and with no knowledge either of her having become a member of Resurrection Chapel.

He wrote his obligatory piece about the women's march, keeping it 'bare bones short' as instructed - since it had to do with a Christian event. Then, of course, gave nary a mention of the largeness of the crowd, which was estimated in the neighborhood of 200,000. "Nothing to reflect glory or credit' was the prevailing watchword; and he did nothing to vary from it, having been sufficiently chastised on his Islamic story to keep within the prescribed lanes.

Nevertheless, he said nothing either about the anti-Muslim pamphlet and the discovered real reason for the rally. Feeling an uncharacteristic sympathy for Amy and, through her - for perhaps the first time - a connection with the Christians as well, he wound up violating a first journalistic principle of not 'going where the story was leading.' Which was a fact not lost on his irate editor.

In reality, with 200,000 women involved, it was unimaginable that word wouldn't slip out one way or another – whether by word of mouth, or other lost pamphlets, or whatever. And at any rate, the editor *did* get wind of it and was livid at Guy Alexander's omission. Swarthy and dark like a thundercloud, despite his unlikely name of *Greenleaf*, his interrogation was particularly caustic. 'How was it possible,' he wanted to know, 'that Alexander, who had researched the Muslims, would not recognize the magnitude of such a story? Here was proof of Christians perhaps seeking to ignite a religious war – a perfect opportunity to shine light on their *true intolerant nature* – and Alexander had said *nothing!*

Hot under the collar and fed up with the hypocrisy, though, Alexander perhaps surprised himself with his edgy response.

"You killed my story on the Muslims before," he said. "So, I assumed you didn't want me to write on them at all!"

To which Editor Greenleaf's "You can't be serious!" response preceded his immediately assigning the follow-on story to a different reporter.

Predictably too, a week after *that* explosive story hit the streets – a story which of course thoroughly trashed the Christian women and their rally – the mailed fist of Islamic justice came crashing down. And it was way worse than even Guy Alexander could have imagined.

Three black hooded jihadists – goons – marched into the *Resurrection Chapel* Sunday service. One sprayed bullets from an automatic weapon into the ceiling, commanding immediate terror; then, from up front, aimed the gun back down at the congregation, sweeping from left to right and daring anyone to move.

His two companions quickly collared Pastor Bowles, dragging him, struggling, from the pulpit. Trying to break free, straining, he raised his head – at which point one of the assailants swung a large blade and in several rapid chopping strokes decapitated him. His head fell with a *thunk* to the floor, followed in swift succession by his wife Patricia's anguished screams and a burst from the automatic weapon which immediately silenced her as well. Others came involuntarily to their feet, only to receive the same fate. And ultimately, scores lay dead and wounded as the Islamic terrorists - *first time visitors to Resurrection Chapel* – exited proudly out the sanctuary's front door.

Afterwards of course, the media declined to label them as Islamic, choosing instead the much less sinister sounding "home grown extremists." And while the crime was so horrific that it had to be reported; and, while some Islamic leaders did express shock and sympathy, they couched their condolences with the *oh so predictable* caveat – 'that the *Resurrection Chapel* had after all produced literature offensive to Allah and the prophet.'

Guy Alexander had no sooner turned off the television with the bulletin reporting the carnage, when a hysterical Eloise was on the other end of the phone, screaming and crying so that he could barely understand her.

"Oh Guy!" she wailed. "Guy, that was my church, and I wrote those pamphlets they're talking about! I should be the one that's dead! I begged Pastor Bowles not to put the church's name on them, but he said Christians had to stand, not hide…."

Guy tried to calm her, but with no noticeable effect, not really knowing what to say or do. He wanted to help her but, deep down in his wavering self-preservationist soul, knew he shouldn't be involved, or even perceived to be. He himself hadn't written the pamphlets, nor had anything to do with them. And yet, he *was* a writer and *had* written negatively about Islam; and knew that if he were linked to her – his former fiancée – he very well might be suspected.

To his credit though, and with self-disgust, he fought it off.

"You can come over here, Eloise," he said, "until we can figure something out."

To which her response was immediately defining of her own true character.

"Oh no, Guy, I couldn't do that to you! I'm so sorry, I just had to talk to someone!" she said. And she hung up.

Which left him at that point about as agitated as he could get. He paced the floor furiously, thinking about calling her back. But then, with each passing minute, it became less of a possibility – as the innate caution began to regain control.

'What was coming?' he thought, 'if the jihadists would make such an attack in broad daylight? In a Sunday church service, no less! Clearly, they had no fear and, in the process, doubtless had intimidated, not just those in *Resurrection Chapel*, but millions across the country. That, of course, had been their intention, also: as the perception that 'if it could happen right outside the Nation's capital, it could happen anywhere' was a powerfully effective one.

Finally, he busied himself, writing an editorial – something which would never be published, and which he wouldn't even submit – venting in a way writers understand, but underneath still retaining the unpleasant taste of cowardice.

Of course, in the days following, the media didn't dwell on the *Resurrection* attack and beheading, instead when even mentioning it, continued with the favorite line that the attackers were *home grown extremists* and not in any way connected to Islam – ignoring the Hamas-like black hoods and the guttural Arabic which the few survivors in the congregation reported hearing, as well as the head-scarfed woman in the back of the church observed videotaping.

The newspapers and television made mention several times, too, that the Resurrection Church should not be considered *mainstream* – that it was not included in any of the major denominations, and was in fact reported by *some* in the neighborhood as being 'a bit odd." The implication being of course that *Resurrection* was a cult where, by definition, odd things were going to happen – which in turn branded the

200,000 women who had received the anti-Muslim packets as misled dupes.

Guy Alexander read the stories in the papers and on the Net, noting the uniformity of the slant and knowing deep in his gut that a cover up was well underway. Knowing that Eloise of all people would never be involved in anything cultish, then impressed, too, at how quickly the story and the never-found assailants simply faded into the woodwork. The more he thought about it - about the near hysteria of level-headed Eloise, together with his conversation with the demonstration leader Amy and the unexplained spiking of his own story, the more his newsman's instincts were again shouting at him that something very big was happening.

So that finally, he went to see his friend, Marine Corps Major General Robert Wilson – the big brother he'd never had, but with whom he'd grown up in tough Baltimore neighborhoods. He was a man who never sugar coated anything and was thus invaluable to a man endeavoring to cover the news. Usually he was gone to some hot spot or other in the world, and it was only recently that Guy had heard that he was at home.

"Alexander!" the big man barked at him with the usual tinge of friendly mocking as Guy came up the walkway.

"Hey!" Guy responded, but with a deference born of genuine respect, not intimidation.

"What are you doing here, Alexander?" the Marine said – large, tomato faced in open necked blue sport shirt and tan khakis. He grabbed Guy's outstretched hand with both of his and pulled him immediately across the threshold.

"I could ask you the same thing. I just heard that you were at home."

"Can't trust anyone with intelligence these days," the Marine groused, then turned immediately serious. "Actually I got dismissed," he said.

"What? Dismissed?" Alexander stared at him.

"Yeah, dismissed! Fired!"

Alexander was incredulous. "What the hell for?"

"Come on!" the now retired Major General inclined his head and led the way from the front door through the living room and into the study.

It was an older home and had been in the Wilson family for at least three generations, kept always military neat by the general's wife Jan who apparently was not in.

"Jan's at her mother's," Wilson said, anticipating the question, as they sat down on facing leather chairs in the small book lined space.

And still not believing what he'd heard at the front door, Guy asked him again. "So what happened?"

To which, the Marine was at first reticent, finally grating out, "let me show you something!" He stood and crossed to the desk - coming back with a sheath of papers.

"These," he said tight-lipped, "are the names of the senior officers dismissed by this administration. Have a look and tell me what you think."

Alexander took the lists from him and thumbed through the pages as directed, his interest growing exponentially. There were names of generals and admirals and majors and colonels and commanders and captains, ranging from the Marines to the Army to the Navy - ten pages in all and including perhaps a hundred and fifty of the elite of the elites. There were everything from commanders of intercontinental ballistic missiles and expeditionary forces to captains of aircraft carriers and submarines and destroyers to heads of electronic attack squadrons and everything in between – in all representing a trove of experience and accomplishment kicked to the curb. And as Guy felt his astonishment transitioning to a raging new anger, Major General (ret) Robert Wilson spoke in a low raspy tone.

"All through world history," he said, "whatever comes after a military purge is never good. And make no mistake about it, this is a purge of unprecedented proportion. Oh, and by the way, every communist regime that's ever risen up has done this very thing on reaching power."

"But why?" Alexander spoke barely above a whisper.

"You tell me, Mister Newsman! Why?"

"Look," Alexander said, "I came to you. But from this that you've shown me, it certainly seems like they've gotten rid of all you guys in order to eliminate the strongest opposition to whatever it is they're planning to do."

"Well yeah, Mister Newsman, I'm with you so far, but do you mean to tell me you didn't know about this before?"

"I knew about Petraeus, of course, and McCrystal, but not a hundred and fifty others. But that's the M.O. of this administration; all you get is bits and pieces."

The General nodded, and Alexander went on. "To your point, though, a communist dictatorship would never be satisfied with a mere eight years in office. By definition, they'd be thinking long term; and unfortunately, I think it goes way beyond just a transition of our system of government."

"How so?" Now, it was the Marine's turn to be on the edge of his chair at attention.

"Look," Guy went on, now in the unusual position of mentoring one of those he considered a mentor. "This guy's not just a Marxist, he's a Muslim; and what I've learned – and to my everlasting shame it's just been learned recently – the Muslims in this country have been working on a quiet, patient fifty year jihad versus our civilization."

And he continued – enumerating and describing all the points in his suppressed article. He spoke in particular of the Saudi's 70 billion dollar investment in building 2000 mosques and the Muslim Brotherhood's early memorandum regarding the strategic goals of eliminating and destroying American civilization from within – to be achieved through a slow, steady process of absorption in which Muslim immigrants would resist assimilation and ultimately impose their values and *sharia* law on American Christians and Jews.

"They've been at this for five decades now," he repeated, "and with this administration in place, maybe they figure it's time to spring the trap door. Seems like if they just remain patient, they're on course to win anyway. But on the other hand, given what you've shown me, maybe a mass round-up of dissidents is on the drawing board right now. And the fact that the administration is hip deep in fomenting phony race riots all over the country could be just a means for giving the President ultimate cover for declaring martial law."

"My God!" Major General Wilson bowed his head, chin on his chest. "I never had any idea the extent of that," he said. And then, "why didn't you folks in the media inform us? You're supposed to be the watchdogs, aren't you?"

"I don't know the exact answer to that," Alexander responded. "Reporters get assigned to stories and don't normally go off on their own like I did. But whether the higher ups – the ones who assign the stories – have been paid off, or in some way coerced, so that news would be presented only in drips and drabs I can't say. But I do know that the Islamic 50 year subterfuge has been masterful."

The two friends sat silent for a minute, considering. Then, when General Wilson spoke, it was with a sad, wistful tone, almost that of a hurt little boy. "I always thought of Islam in America as being kind of comical, with Nation of Islam spokesmen like Elijah Muhammed running around espousing mother planes and flying saucers transporting black guys to and from Mecca," he said.

"Yeah, I know," Alexander returned grimly, "but after the immigration law was changed and the heavy hitters flooded in here – the seven million or so true followers of Allah and Mohammed from the Middle East – they've used that perception to their advantage. Hiding behind the seemingly comical image while establishing a couple of thousand nonprofit charities, many of which have financed jihad and terrorism all over the world."

Again the two were silent – until once again the Marine spoke.

"Alexander, why did you come to me with this today?"

"Did you hear about the pastor being beheaded in Arlington the other day?" Guy answered his question with one of his own.

"Yeah, and his wife and half the congregation mowed down besides! I saw it on the tube, but haven't heard much about it since. Did they catch the guys who did it?"

"You mean the quote, unquote *home grown extremists*? No, and I doubt they ever will, given their powerful connections.

But anyway, you asked me why I came, and that was part of the reason. There's a Christian group operating out there, trying to get the truth out about the Muslims, however late it may be. And the church that got hit – *Resurrection Chapel* and the pastor - were a part of it. I don't know how extensive the group is, or what effect the attack will have had, but I thought you might have some ideas for helping or protecting them. That is before I learned about your situation, and these (pointing to the list) others."

"Oh man!" Wilson groaned. "We're all mostly in a state of shock, I think. And what with the NSA surveillance no doubt focused on us, I don't see how we can mount much of a campaign at all – though you can be sure now that I'll be thinking about it."

"Dammit!" Alexander swore bleakly. Dammit anyway!"

"Yeah, I know," the General said, standing then and putting a hand on Guy's shoulder. "But always remember, Alexander, America ain't dead until she's dead!"

"I'm sorry if I put you under more suspicion by coming here," Guy said. "I had no idea!"

"Well, I hope by comin' here, you didn't put *yourself* in more jeopardy as well. Next time, maybe just write a note; but, however you do it, keep me up to date. Please! And I'll be doin' what I can – as soon as I can. I promise!"

CHAPTER FOURTEEN

Chrislam

"*I still believe so strongly in interfaith cooperation between our Christianity and Islam. Of course, I had an unfortunate experience, but I was simply targeted by some bad apples. That can happen in any endeavor where humankind is involved.*

"*Why, I've heard that the great and famous pastor, Rick Warren, believes similarly — that love and cooperation are the keys and that, in fact, we and the Muslims worship the same God. A belief which flies in the face of my dear ex-wife Amy's outrageous contention that Islam is a demonic cult. Pastor Warren believes so strongly that he has established an outreach group called "King's Way" and was rewarded with the opportunity to offer the invocation at the President's inauguration.*

"*I know that there are seventy-five or a hundred other churches which have come together in an organization titled "Faith Shared" — also for the purpose of reaching out to our Islamic brothers and sisters. And of course, the wonderful idyllic goal is the celestial ideal of "Chrislam" - a true marriage of the two faiths and a lying down of the lion with the lamb. I know that back in Fort Wayne, the Presbyterian Church was involved in this ministry; and it had been my fervent hope to involve our church similarly. Things just happened too fast; but maybe, after I've been here awhile, and have a little more influence, I'll be able to nudge my new boss, our senior pastor, towards "Chrislam" as well. I certainly hope so. And what a blessed day that will be!"*

–Reverend Benjamin Brown

Benjamin Brown had found a new home. He'd caught on as a youth pastor in a Congregational Church in the town of Marion, about half way between Fort Wayne and Indianapolis. Of course, it was a step down from being a lead pastor; still he was surprisingly upbeat, going through the paces with the youngsters, while freed from sermon preparations and the various administrative duties of before.

Now, he was finally healing, too, from the split with Amy – whom he was still trying to forgive – missing her less all the time and beginning to notice young women in the congregation, who he believed in turn were noticing him. He tried to repress the fact that Amy had been right about the Muslims, at least the ones who had come to their church. Nevertheless, the loss of the church remained a dark cloud and he continued shamed and embarrassed by having been made the fool.

There were unguarded times, too, when a residual fear would rise up, and the shocking image of the planted nude Arab girl in the rectory would return. The subterranean plotting involved in placing her there, then having her perform at the precise time of the Imam's arrival continued to gnaw at him. He just couldn't quite get a handle on such a malevolent evil. He had been so hopeful with the arrival of the new Arab congregants and had considered the Imam to be a friend – a man who ultimately had threatened and blackmailed him right out of his church. And he shuddered at the memory, while trying to press on towards the sunshine.

His parents mentioned that Amy had phoned, trying to get in touch with him. But then, he was more than satisfied to learn of his mother's hanging up the phone. 'That ship has sailed,' he thought, 'and good riddance' - at no time even considering that, as his one-time *co-pastor*, she might be entitled to know what actually had become of *their* church.

Now he was settled into the transferring of his brand of *Christian reasonableness/* i.e. Christian political correctness to the crop of young minds put in his charge each week. And he felt good about it, and good about himself.

But then one day, all too soon, the dark specter returned and blotted out the sun. He had just bicycled up to his apartment complex, which was only blocks from the church; and, tired, he scarcely noticed a parked black panel van. Dismissing it as belonging to some utility enterprise or other, he was thus completely taken aback when two swarthy Mid-eastern types leapt out and accosted him.

"Benjamin Brown?"

"Yes," he said uncertainly, leaning the bike against the apartment building wall.

"You need to come with us!" The voice was low but certain; and the speaker – who was the man closest to Benjamin and approaching – brushed his gray sports coat to the side, revealing a handgun stuck somewhat incongruously in the waistband of his dark slacks.

"What? I don't understand . . ."

"Hurry up and get in the van. We don't have much time!"

"Much time for what?"

Now both the men were on him, each taking an arm and then propelling him in through the opened passenger side door. After which, he sat between them on the undivided front seat as they sped off down the road. The speaker, who sat on the passenger side, kept the pistol thrust into Benjamin's ribs and his cold, business-like attitude left no doubt of his willingness if necessary to pull the trigger.

"Look," Benjamin tried again, "what's this about? I think you've made some mistake. I'm just a youth pastor in a church."

"Infidel liar!" was the angry retort. "Be quiet and you will see!"

Then, he was further surprised when, within only a few miles, they pulled into a motel parking lot. They all got out, and, with Benjamin once again flanked by the two goons, proceeded only a few steps to a ground floor room. A single knock brought an immediate opening of the door; and then he was face to face again with *old friend* Imam Abdul Rahmin.

"Benjamin!" he said, at once emoting the old enthusiasm and oily charm. "Sorry for the rough treatment, but it is an emergency and I need your immediate help!"

"What emergency?" Benjamin heard himself say again coldly.

"Come in! Come in!" the Imam said. "Sit down and let me get you a nice drink of water!"

"I don't want a drink of water," Benjamin said, nevertheless sitting as he was told.

It was a small room with a bed, TV, table and two straight chairs. And after Benjamin sat on one of the chairs, the Imam sat nearby on the bed; while the two captors remained standing by the now closed door.

"Benjamin," the Imam began, "we've had some rather distressing news. The woman who used to be your wife – Amy, I believe – is suspected of being a leader of a virulently anti-Islamic Christian group. In fact, one of our associates at our Fort Wayne mosque identified her at a recent rally held in Washington D.C."

Benjamin started. "Amy?" he said.

"Yes, as a matter of course, we Muslims run surveillance video of all the Christian rallies held in the Capitol, then study them afterwards."

"But why?" Benjamin said. "They're just religious people – like you and me!"

"Not always true," the Imam replied. "In this case, they were distributing pamphlets, not to the honor of your God, but for the purpose of dishonoring ours. But at any rate, we just want to talk with Amy, and any of the other leaders we can identify – just to let them know that in fact our aims are peaceful. That there is in fact no malice."

"Well, I don't know where Amy is. I haven't talked to her at all since the divorce."

"But you could find her, right? Could telephone to her family members – her mother and father – and they would tell you how to reach her."

"Maybe, I could," Benjamin said, no less affronted than before, "but I don't see why I should want to. This is America and, if her opinion is different from yours, well so be it!"

"Now Benjamin," the Imam went on smoothly, "of course, we know this is America and that everyone has a right to their free speech. We just want to correct slander where it exists. We only want to reason with her in the spirit of love and cooperation – so that perhaps she and her group will recognize our truly peaceful intent."

At which point, Benjamin became again like butter in his hands, melting at the reminder of the love and cooperation they'd discussed before, opting readily for the gentler path as of course the Imam knew that he would. Benjamin was after all enamored of himself at the core, and saw his role always as leading others importantly towards a non-confrontational *lollipop* world.

"Really?" he said, wide eyed, so that it was a wonder the Imam and his standing-by goons didn't break out laughing at his weakness. "You really just want to talk with her?"

"Well yes, Benjamin," the Imam soothed. "Just a little talk."

"But, why the urgency?" he ventured plaintively, "if it's just going to be a little talk."

"Because Benjamin," and now the Imam seemed straining to be patient, "because, as you people here in the States would say, we don't want her and her people to *damage our brand*. We want only to understand and be understood – so that eventually we might be accepted as full-fledged Americans."

At which point, Benjamin was softened completely, as more tenets of his idealism resurrected and streamed again through his mind. 'What after all would he feel and do if he were an immigrant – a stranger in a strange land? And wouldn't he have a craving to understand and be understood? And also, might not his methods towards achieving those goals seem awkward as well?'

Still he hesitated - hesitated at the idea of calling Amy, or her parents. Until finally, running out of patience, the Imam for a moment reverted – reminding Benjamin of whose decision it really was.

"Look Benjamin," he said more sternly, "as I told you, many of us do deem this urgent. We are in a hurry and so you must act now. Otherwise, I can't guarantee that certain information won't find its way into your new church situation. And I'm sure you know the information to which I refer."

So that Benjamin flushed – as once again his *pie in the sky* idealism came up hard against the implacable wall of Islamic reality.

On the phone, Amy's mother was certainly more cordial than his mother had been when Amy had called looking for him. But he believed it was a result of his invoking the mentor, Brother Kyle's name. 'Brother Kyle had suggested he call,' he lied – with what he thought grimly was a touch of genius. And sure enough, her mother gave him Amy's number, adding also that Amy was living now in an apartment in Indianapolis.

"Oh, where would that be?" he asked, hoping not to have to talk to Amy and ultimately deceive her. However, her mother demurred, not willing to go that far and suggesting he go ahead and call her, the implication being of course that it would be up to Amy to divulge further information.

He hung up, having written the phone number down. But then immediately, the Imam was at him again, questioning. 'Who was Brother Kyle?' he wanted to know. And with a certain unexplained foreboding, Benjamin told him – that Brother Kyle had been Amy's closest faculty friend and advisor at the Bible School she'd attended.

"Hmm, interesting!" was the Imam's response, as he scribbled a note – doubtless Brother Kyle's name – on his little memo pad. "Well now go ahead and call her, Benjamin," he said. "And remember she is your *EX!* wife; and also that we have no intention of harming her – just talking. And for now, just find out where she lives. You don't have to set a specific time or date."

He punched in the number, feeling a rising anxiety – so that he barely recognized his own voice when responding to her greeting.

"Benjamin," she said, surprised. "Is that you?"

"Yes, Amy," he managed. "Brother Kyle suggested it might be a good thing if we talked, and your mother gave me your number."

"Which is a little different from the way your mom responded to me," she replied with her forever directness.

"Well, I'm sorry for that," he said. "Where do you live? Do you think I could come by sometime?"

"Well, I live in the Westbury Apartments, number 105. But on second thought, it would probably be better if we had our little talk on neutral ground. Say some place like Starbucks."

"Sure," he said. "I could pick you up and take you, or we could just meet."

"Just meet," she said.

"Any particular time of day?" he said, secure in the knowledge that he already had her address, but nevertheless having to endure the scowl and wagging finger of the Imam.

"Well, how about tomorrow at three o'clock?"

"Sure Amy," he said, "three o'clock tomorrow at Starbucks will be fine."

Then after he'd hung up, he stopped the Imam in mid-flight. "I got the address," he said; and then, within minutes, they were back in the van and on the way over.

Now, however, the Imam rode up front with the others, while Benjamin was relegated to half sitting, half lying on a padded mattress in the rear. Then afterwards, when they reached Indianapolis and he told them how to get to the apartment complex, he in turn was informed he would be going to the door to draw Amy outside. Or alternatively, if she weren't yet home, they would wait in the van until she arrived.

Feeling dirtier than ever in his life, he endured the ride, then on arrival was thinking of bolting when the Imam reached back an object to him. It was in fact a blown up nude photo of the girl from *the incident*. He could see she was on his old bed in the Fort Wayne rectory, lying on her stomach and gazing at a framed picture in her hands – a serious picture of him in the pulpit addressing the flock – a picture which had strangely disappeared just prior to his leaving.

"We have several copies of this photo of the girl," the Imam informed, "enough for wide distribution. So, I suggest that if you want to continue your valuable ministry to the young people, you will comply with our simple requests. And again Benjamin, remember! She is your EX-wife – the one who humiliated you!"

He went to the apartment door. She was surprised – blond, young, more vibrant even than he had remembered. He said there was something he needed to show her. She came outside. The goons grabbed her, and in her case applied cuffs and a gag. And in literally a couple of minutes, they were back on the road, now with the once married couple together again on the soiled rear mattress.

Gagged as she was, Amy couldn't speak to Benjamin, but her eyes conveyed a full spectrum of anger, wonderment, hurt and disdain. So that finally, he didn't look at her anymore. However, by then it was too late, as he was already drowning in self-loathing and regret.

Finally, after they'd gotten onto Interstate 69 and were heading North, he found his voice sufficiently to ask. "Where are you taking us? To Fort Wayne?" Hoping perhaps his question would cause her to think of him as a victim as well.

"Oh Benjamin," the Imam said solicitously, "don't worry yourself. No, we are taking a little trip to Dearborn in Michigan – to the Islamic Center of all of North America. You will both love it there!"

He chuckled as he said it; the two henchmen chimed in laughing; and Amy's sudden look of terror penetrated to Benjamin's soul.

Later in the evening, as they entered Dearborn, the Imam served as tour guide. "This is one of our notorious "no go zones," Benjamin," he said – "a designation which for political reasons we of course deny. But where in reality police and firemen don't enter; infidels walk the streets at their peril; and our glorious *sharia* law absolutely prevails."

Out of the van afterwards and inside a large warehouse, they were shepherded through the darkness to a far lighted corner, with Amy unsteady and stumbling after the cramped ride, and Benjamin with rising unnamed dread.

CHAPTER FIFTEEN

New Intelligence Committee Member – Close Ties to Muslim Brotherhood

House Minority Leader Nancy Pelosi recently appointed Rep Andre Carson (D-IN) to a coveted position on the House Permanent Select Committee on Intelligence. This panel is charged with oversight of the United States' most sensitive national intelligence capabilities and operations. These include any directed at Islamist supremacists seeking to impose worldwide – through violent and, where necessary, through stealthy forms of jihad – the totalitarian program they call shariah.

"…it is therefore problematic and potentially detrimental to the national security that Rep Carson has extensive and longstanding ties to organizations and individuals associated with the Muslim Brotherhood. As established in a **dossier** *and* **video** *released today (Feb 25,2015)by the Center for Security Policy, the Indiana congressman has an extensive record of involvement with, support of and support from a virtual Who's Who of Brotherhood front organizations in America and leading figures in the jihad movement in this country. The dossier makes it clear that, as a group, they have*

*a documented history of serving as unregistered foreign agents,
engaging in material support for terrorism and possessing direct
ties to the Brotherhood's Palestinian franchise, Hamas, a
designated terrorist organization.*"

–Center for Security Policy
Washington, D.C.
(February 25, 2015)

After the visit to his friend, *former* Major General Robert
Wilson, Guy Alexander returned to the newspaper, feeling
more at loose ends than even before. He felt he was a man
knowing a catastrophic crash was about to happen, and yet with
no means of stopping it. He couldn't think of anyone else he
might talk with – though still feeling the need. There were, of
course, his political contacts on the Hill, but that was always a
crap shoot – since with politicians, one seldom, if ever, knew
which side they were really on. The Saudis had spent 70 billion
petro dollars on mosques across the country and Alexander had
no doubt that a few left over "pocket change" millions had
been dispersed currying political favor as well. One woman,
much touted to be a future presidential candidate and revered as
a women's rights advocate, reputedly had accepted 25 million
for her *family foundation* already – and notwithstanding the Saudis
leading the world in female repression.

At the newspaper, he was immediately assigned a trip to
Indiana to cover a developing story on a so-called *religious
freedom* bill. Proponents were seeking to protect Christian
businesses from having to compromise principles in serving gay
weddings. Which the LGBT (lesbian/gay/bi-sexual/
transgender) alliance was opposing with all the considerable
loathing hatred they could bring to bear. And while his editor
did not spare the sarcasm in assigning Guy the story, noting
that he should be able to do a 'decent job' of reporting since
there'd be no Muslim bias involved, Alexander was thoroughly
conflicted, nevertheless.

Because of his homosexual dalliances, he had on occasion
thought about gay marriage (as a concept) and rejected it totally
because the idea of gay couples raising children seemed to him a

case of taking one half of children's lives away from them just so the "parents" might feel themselves whole. But beyond that, he thought, given the President's outspoken support of gay rights, this proliferation of another whole genre of street uprisings would be added to the ongoing race riots to increase the impetus for the suspected declaration of martial law. Which led him, and regardless the editor, right back to his original supposition of the looming threat of sharia.

Alexander paid a last visit to his desk at the paper to transfer phone messages while he was out of town; put his plane ticket in his briefcase; then headed back to his apartment to pack. However, there, he was met at the front doorstep by two agents from the FBI.

It was not completely unexpected, given the Administration's unprecedented paranoia regarding leaks, and the more aggressive than ever before effort to get journalists to give up sources. But then very soon, he realized that this was something else.

He asked if they could just go inside and interview him there, since he was scheduled to be at the airport in a couple of hours. But they refused, stating that he needed to go with them to their office downtown – leaving him equal parts irritated, curious and vaguely frightened.

They were middle aged, olive skinned, in characteristic dark hats and gray trench coats. And immediately, when one introduced himself as Agent al-Sahmin, warning bells went off in Alexander's head. At once, he demanded to see credentials, wondering if in fact they were Islamists who had somehow gotten wind of his relationship with Eloise and were doing their own investigating. However, when they complied and he saw that the second agent's name was Rodriguez, he relaxed somewhat, remembering the Bureau's recent campaign to hire minorities, particularly Muslims and Hispanics.

He asked how long they might be and they were non-committal. Then, when he started to reach in his inside pocket for his cell phone, they snapped to attention in such a way that he stopped his hand in mid-flight.

"What, are ya nuts?" he said, as frustration boiled over. "I've gotta call the newspaper and tell them to get somebody else to fly to Indiana!"

In the car heading back downtown, they continued tight-lipped though; and it wasn't until they'd entered the glass and steel building and arrived in a third floor office that he finally found out what it was about.

"Do you know a young woman by the name of Amy Shiloh?"

"No, I don't think so."

"Well, that's interesting. We have pictures of you having coffee with her at a sidewalk café called *The Elephant and Castle.*"

"What?" he said, thoroughly shocked.

"We've got pictures of you . . . "

"I heard what you said! But why the hell does it matter whom I have coffee with? This is still America in case you haven't noticed. And yes, now that you mention it, I did have a cup of coffee with a girl named Amy, though I never did get her last name."

"Well, were you trying to get her last name?"

"Now, what kind of stupid question is that? Of course, I was trying to get her last name. She was a good lookin' woman; I was bored covering the stupid parade; and I was hitting on her. So what?"

"But she wouldn't give you her name?"

"No, or her phone number. And here's a news flash for you, too. I don't always get what I want!"

"Yeah, well here's a news flash for you as well, Mister Alexander. Everything's not about you. It really isn't! We're investigating Amy Shiloh and all the leaders of that march and the members of the Resurrection Church in Alexandria as a probable hate group."

"Oh really!" Alexander said, his voice laced with sarcasm, and wishing later on that he'd just remained silent. "They're the hate group? I thought the Resurrection pastor was the one who got beheaded, and his congregation members the ones who got shot."

"Well, they instigated it with the hate speech contained in the pamphlets they passed out."

"Hate speech? I read one of those pamphlets and I didn't detect any hate speech at all. It seemed like a pretty straightforward description of Islamic goals in America. But, I guess Christians aren't supposed to know about such things, eh?"

"Tell us about your relationship with Miss Eloise Turner. We know that you're involved with her and also that she's a member of the Resurrection church."

"Well in that case, I think that you should arrest her right away. Imagine in America, a person choosing to be a member of a particular church! Yes, I know Eloise. In fact, I used to be engaged to her; but then she went off to Europe for quite awhile and it fizzled out. I'm not much good at long distance relationships, I'm afraid."

"When's the last time you saw her?"

"Oh, a few weeks ago."

"But, she called you."

"Well, you say it like you know it, so I suppose you're got the NSA on me. Yes, she called me right after her pastor got beheaded. She was hysterical, as you might expect, and I tried to calm her down. But I haven't heard from her since."

"Well for that matter, nobody's heard from her. But, did you know she wrote the pamphlets – the one in particular we were talking about, that they passed out at the demonstration?"

"She mentioned that she was helping with some writing, but I don't know the extent of it."

"Mister Alexander," Agent al-Sahmin, the equal opportunity Muslim agent addressed him then (Agent Rodriguez having done the questioning to that point). "We have information from your employer that recently you were involved in very extensive research into Islam in America – that you in fact wrote an article which the paper spiked as being too incendiary. So that, given your involvement with Ms Turner and Ms Shiloh, we're going to be holding you for awhile – until we see how this all plays out."

"Holding me?"

"Well, charging you. With suspicion of fomenting hate crimes."

* * * *

Reaching the lighted corner of the vast, otherwise dark warehouse, Benjamin and Amy found themselves in what amounted to a mini television studio – naturally heightening fears as images of videotaped hostages had been much in the news. Klieg lights were switched on suddenly; two more men emerged from the shadows rolling forward tall television cameras, while one of the original goons stepped forward to position two high backed chairs side by side in the center.

Then, Imam Abdul-Rahmin spoke in his most soothing manner. "Now Benjamin," he said, "and you young lady, I know that you're feeling some fear and uncertainty right now, but really it's not what it appears. In fact, we are just wanting to make a little movie here to advance the cause of understanding between our peoples. You know, Benjamin, you and I have discussed these concerns together in the past; and you can be assured that you'll be contributing to that cause.

"Just to put you at ease, too, we've decided to title our little film, "The Love Birds" – in honor of your past relationship. And you young lady, now that you're nicely calmed down, we're going to release your bonds and ask you just to sit on one of the chairs, up there next to Benjamin."

From behind, the cuffs were taken off and the gag removed; and, not really knowing what else to do, she went ahead and walked up with Benjamin to the chairs. After they were seated, one of the cameramen came forward to place fake gold tiaras topped with little crosses on their heads, giving them the appearance of homecoming royalty. Then the Imam distracted by requesting that Benjamin rest a hand on Amy's trembling shoulder; while the second cameraman actually finished the preparations by belting each of them to the chairs from behind.

"Okay, I'm going to leave you love birds to it now," the Imam said. "I have more important things to do, but have fun! Believe me, you'll be well taken care of." And he walked off into the darkness, his footsteps echoing fadingly from the concrete floor. And with his leaving, a palpable departure, too, of any level of reason.

The two cameramen trucked their cameras forward from separate angles; and immediately one of the original goons, now in a black hood and coveralls, walked over and positioning himself so the camera *could see,* grabbed Benjamin's left ear and, with a very sharp serrated blade, promptly sawed it off.

Benjamin howled, his anguish echoing in the huge empty warehouse, trying but unable to stand up, as Amy screamed then as well. Benjamin reached up, clamping his hand over where his ear had been, sobbing uncontrollably; while the cameras' red lights indicated their continued rolling.

The black hood bent down to pick up the severed ear, then held it up, kissed it for the camera and presented it to Amy – who brushed it away angrily. At which point, too, it was as if a different switch had been turned on; and afterwards an otherworldly calm seemed to descend upon Amy, which in turn radiated outward. "Jesus is Lord," she said. And the black hood, who underneath was the same punk he'd always been, lashed out with the knife, slicing her cheek.

"Allah be praised!" he howled. "Allah be praised!"

Amy raised a hand to her cheek, but otherwise didn't respond, unlike Benjamin who continued to sob. Then, the other goon who had come with them in the car re-emerged as well, also wearing a black hood.

"All you have to do," he said to Amy in a thick accent, "is give to us the names of the other pastors involved in that cursed Washington rally, and we will make a quick end to all of this."

"Jesus is Lord!" she replied. And he reached over, grabbing her blond hair in the front and, with his own sharp knife, hacked it off down to the scalp.

"It's a real pity, Missy," he rasped, "for a pretty girl like yourself to have her good looks spoiled over something so unimportant."

"Jesus is Lord!" she said. At which point, Benjamin let out another howl as the other goon had slid a small butcher's block over, held Benjamin's hand on it and chopped off a finger. "What do you think there woman?" he said, looking over at Amy. "Are you just going to let your man suffer, you typical American bitch?"

"Jesus is Lord," she repeated quietly. So that he immediately chopped off another finger, and Benjamin became hysterical.

"Please stop!" he screamed. "Please don't hurt me anymore! I'll do anything! I'll praise Allah! I'll praise Allah to the sky!"

The black hood let go of his wrist. "Oh that's very different, Pastor Benjamin!" he said, also lowering the knife to his side. "Very good! And do you renounce Jesus Christ as well?"

"Oh yes!" Benjamin gasped. "I do! My faith was never so strong anyway."

"Oh no, Benjamin!" Amy cried. And *her* assailant reached out to slash her forehead.

"Not so pretty now!" he snarled.

"Jesus is Lord!" she returned. And further enraged, with a fast upward stroke, he cut off the tip of her nose.

"It will be beyond surgical repair very soon!" he said.

"Jesus is Lord!" she said.

At which point, Benjamin's goon pushed the chopping block over in front of Amy, then turned Benjamin's chair so that he would have a better view.

"Now Pastor Benjamin, my new Muslim brother, you will get a better view of how we deal with the infidel."

Amy's thug held one of her hands up on the block then and, grinding down on the knife, removed her thumb. To which her measured "Jesus is Lord" further enraged him, so that he then swiftly chopped off one finger after the other until they all were gone.

"Now," he said, breathing heavily and with somewhat lessened confidence, "shall we start on your other hand, or will you tell us the names of the other people that were involved?"

But now, there was no response, as in fact she had passed out. Smelling salts were fetched; then, when she'd regained consciousness, the proposition was put before her still again.

"Jesus is Lord!" she intoned. Whereupon in a final fit of rage, her assailant raised what was left of her hair in the back and from behind brought his knife up under her chin, severing her neck and ultimately removing her head. The cameras were trucked in for a close up of the spurting blood; and the butcher purposefully reached out the trophy – the hair with Amy's attached head - to Benjamin.

"She – I must admit my dear brother in Allah," he said, "was what an American male should aspire to be."

Benjamin didn't want to take it from him, withdrawing his uninjured hand, but the Islamist terrorist insisted. "No Benjamin," he said, "it is for you. She was your wife. Take it! You must take it!"

Finally Benjamin reached and grasped what were left of Amy's soft tresses for a last time - holding on, and with her head knocking against his leg, as now unbelted from the chair, he was led stumblingly, unknowingly into the darkness beyond the cameras.

"Almost finished now, my dear brother in Allah," his assailant said soothingly, sympathetically, eliciting still another plaintive sob. "Almost finished, my dear Benjamin!"

They had him sit down then in the darkness on what appeared to be a board lying on the floor, encouraging him to lie back and, at the same time, disengaging his hand from Amy's hair, which by that time he didn't want to let go. Nevertheless, *both* voices were soothing in persuasion now, so that he finally complied.

"Just rest for a little while, dear brother Benjamin. We know that you have been through a lot!"

Still dazed, he stretched out, while aware that for whatever reason they were positioning him. One of his new friends, who were so solicitous, even insisted on his stretching his arms out to the sides – 'in order to better relax.' And it wasn't until spikes were driven simultaneously into his wrists that the full horror penetrated his pain shocked brain. He was being CRUCIFIED!

He screamed and squirmed involuntarily, kicking his legs; but that only intensified the blinding pain shooting from his wrists up into his brain. So that very soon, he stopped his struggling. And another big spike was driven through his crossed feet.

Finished, they raised the crucifix then with him on it, already gasping for every breath – setting the end down into an adapted slot in the floor. Klieg lights and cameras were shifted. And the cameras rolled.

CHAPTER SIXTEEN

Silence, Accomplice to Injustice

People ask me if I have some kind of death wish, to keep saying the things I do. The answer is no: I would like to keep living. However, some things must be said and there are times when silence becomes an accomplice to injustice."

—Ayaan Hirsi Ali, *Infidel*

Dying as a martyr is sometimes portrayed as something glorious, but in general people don't line up for the opportunity. Still the few dozen leaders who had met in St. Louis - colleagues of the beheaded Pastor Bowles – were in a way bolstered by his death; strengthened in their belief that the path they'd chosen was necessary and right.

The select few working with them like Amy and Eloise were pretty much of the same mind, too. Still after Pastor Bowles' death and the attack on *Resurrection Chapel*, it was agreed not to hold further large strategy meetings, in order to avoid at all costs an event which might take them all. Further, communications between the cell churches were limited to regular mail rather than phone calls, e-mails or text messages; and a failsafe policy which had been agreed to at the St. Louis meeting became more relevant. Should any of them feel their position compromised at any time, they would immediately mail an empty envelope of warning to all of the others. Thus, each member kept a stack of pre- stamped and addressed envelopes ready to go at all times, the receipt of one being a signal to proceed with extreme caution, or even disappear.

When Amy didn't show up at the Bible College for work, Brother Kyle tried phoning her, then went by her apartment. However, there his concern was only heightened by the presence of her red Toyota in the driveway, but a failure to respond to his knocking on her door.

He prevailed upon the apartment manager to check on her; but inside, there was no sign except for some chopped up vegetables on the counter indicating that she *had* been home. A call to her parents on the farm yielded no news either; but then, back outside with the manager, one of Amy's neighbors – an orange haired woman out walking a white poodle – spoke up suddenly, unexpectedly.

"Are you looking for that nice young lady who lives here?" she said. "I saw her being escorted out last night by three kind of rough looking men. Well, two of them were rough looking. I couldn't see very well, but it was almost as if they were dragging her. It all happened so fast, I wasn't even sure what I saw. And then they drove off fast in some sort of black truck."

Immediately, for Brother Kyle, it was like a bomb going off. Somehow, he managed to thank the woman; the apartment manager called to alert the police; and, after returning to the campus to mail the four dozen empty envelopes, he returned home just long enough to collect his wife. Then, as also agreed upon in St. Louis, being the one at the point of attack, he immediately disappeared underground.

The following day, when two swarthy gentlemen came looking for him in the school office, no one had seen him. Nor were there any witnesses to a subsequent evening firebombing of his home.

The next Sunday, too, at the college chapel service, right after praise and worship and just before the Chaplain began his message, there was a peculiar buzzing noise. Some looked around, believing it to be a cell phone. But, the volume increased drastically, deafeningly, as audio people and ushers struggled to find the source.

Then the lights went out and total panic ensued, with people stumbling out of their seats and over one another. Many were trampled and injured, pouring and tumbling out of the front doors.

Police, firemen and ambulances arrived; and investigations were conducted for days afterwards with no definitive results. All belongings left behind were carefully screened with no device ever detected responsible for the devastating sound. Then, after the inspections, the various items were placed in the school's *lost and found* – with claims made on an honor basis. And perhaps most telling was one young woman's grieving over a damaged pretty blue box she'd brought to church after an early, pre-service shopping trip to the mall.

* * * *

In Washington D.C., Guy Alexander continued in jail as, in an unprecedented move, his newspaper declined to pay his bail. Rather, a front page article was run, filled with innuendo regarding his possible connections to suspected members of the hate mongering *Resurrection Chapel* Christian cult. Which, of course, served to place the paper in the forefront of defenders of the brave new world of multi-culturalism. While also, in the upside down logic of the *politically correct*, managing to portray the still at large perpetrators of the *Resurrection* attack as the ultimate victims.

The bail had been set at a not astronomical amount of $15,000; and in the early afternoon of the second day, it was paid by a tight-lipped and perturbed ex-Marine Major General.

"Damn Alexander!" Robert Wilson said as Guy made his way out into the front lobby.

"Damn is right!"

They walked outside and Guy breathed in the fresh air. "Ah," he said wryly, "to be a free man!"

"So, how did it go down?"

"Oh man! The FBI came to my apartment. Actually, they were waiting for me when I got home from work."

"And what'd they say?"

"They didn't say much of anything at first – just that I needed to go downtown with them. And I figured it was just another case of the Administration hassling journalists and trying to determine sources. They were dark skinned guys though and one of them gave his name as Agent al-Sahmin, so that I was suspicious and asked for their ID's. Which checked out okay; but then later in their building, they asked questions I wasn't expecting.

"In fact, they started asking me about that Christian women's rally and about one of the woman leaders – a woman named Amy whom I had a cup of coffee with, when I got bored out of my scull watching the parade go by.

"She and her people were passing out leaflets, actually exposing the Muslim takeover; and the FBI guys claimed that was what precipitated the attack on the church over in Alexandria and the beheading of the pastor. Turns out, too, that because my former fiancée Eloise is a member of that church and actually penned the flyers, then of course I must be an accomplice and, get this, a suspect in the fomenting of hate crimes as well!"

"Well yeah, that's pretty much what was all over the front page of the paper."

"Oh yeah, I wondered how you knew to bail me out. And by the way, thanks!"

They'd reached Wilson's pickup truck by then and were momentarily silent.

"Yeah, well about the Muslim FBI agent," the General spoke again, once they were onto the beltway, "I don't know if you remember when Robert Mueller was the Bureau's chief, but he got so enamored with Islam that he hired a bunch of them."

"Well I didn't remember that specifically, but I do know they're all through the government now, not just in the FBI, but in the CIA. And not only that, but get this! I just heard that one guy who's supposedly in tight with the Muslim Brotherhood, is up for election to the board of the NRA. If you can imagine that!"

"Man! The National Rifle Association!" Wilson looked shocked. "Then, the terrorists will have access to the name and address of every serious gun owner in the country - if it finally comes to that!"

"Precisely," Alexander said. "Precisely what I'm thinking!"

They were silent again for a minute, considering – until Alexander again spoke up.

"Look Robert," he said, "you know I'm grateful, but I'm plenty worried that you've turned the spotlight on yourself now as well."

"At ease, Alexander," the Major General snapped. "I'll handle all the heat the *wuzzies* want to throw at me! And it's high time all us guys were standing up anyway. We're like a ticking time bomb, and we're needing to go off!"

"Yeah," Guy said doubtfully, "except how are you going to organize without being monitored? And what media's going to cover it?"

"Look," his friend said, ignoring the questions, "about that bail – I'd expect you to jump it, if you need to. And don't worry about it! I know you can do a whole lot more good outside than in. I want to help – and, if it comes to that, I can afford it."

Then, after pulling over in front of Guy's apartment, the big Marine surprised him by getting out of the truck and walking over to Alexander's dark sedan parked in the driveway. Without hesitation, he lay down, then pulled himself underneath, grunting as he wrestled with something while Alexander stood alongside. Then in a minute or two, he emerged with a small black box with wires attached.

"We had to use one of these little gizmos once in Jordan when we were tracking one of our own – one of our own Muslims!" he said.

He placed a hand on Guy's shoulder. "Don't be real surprised," he said, his eyes now mirroring his concern, "if they've been in your apartment as well - while you've been away. They're obviously very interested.

He handed over the device, then spoke even more somberly. "Guy, I've got some intel from one of my sources that ISIS has set up camps in Mexico, only a few miles from the Southern border. And when you couple that with the millions of Muslims already in the country you've spoken of, and many of them doubtless jihadists, it's not a stretch to envision hundreds of simultaneous beheadings. Which certainly would be another pretext for our Muslim commander in chief to declare martial law along with his continued dictatorship."

Alexander stared at him, thinking that that possibility certainly trumped his own concerns relative to the racist and homosexual rioting – or was perhaps just the completing of the whole.

Wilson climbed back up in his truck, then dropped one last bombshell before driving away.

"There was a video on U-Tube this morning that'll get your attention, too" he said. "A beheading and a crucifixion! Already! Apparently right here in the States!"

Alexander entered the apartment then, and immediately it was as if he'd entered someone else's place. Things weren't in their usual spots; and then in the den, he saw that his computer was gone from the desk, as well as a drawer full of files.

At which point, feeling violated, but also with a rising anger, he went without further hesitation and threw clothes and personal effects into a bag and made his departure.

Outside in the lobby, he accessed his mailbox for perhaps the last time, stuffing the several envelopes into his coat pocket. Then took Interstate 95 South, and it wasn't until he reached Fredericksburg and stopped for gas that he began to worry that he might be without funds. It was easy to envision the FBI freezing his accounts. However, when he tried a credit card at the pump, he was vastly relieved when it worked, thinking nevertheless that he should find an ATM somewhere soon and draw out whatever he could get.

Then, calming, he reminded himself that, since there was absolutely nothing on his computer, or in his files, that was incriminating, save of course the already acknowledged research on Islam, it would be premature for them to take such drastic action. Maybe . . .?

Sitting in a diner, waiting for his meal, he remembered the letters in his pocket and was surprised then to discover one with no return address but graced with Eloise's distinct handwriting. He opened it, aware of his elevated heart rate. Then read:

*My Dearest Guy: I'm so sorry! I know I've probably gotten
you into trouble. I just can't deal with all of this. I have friends
- from before - in France, who are living now in Tahiti. I'm
going to be with them and will send you an address. If you ever
decide, please COME!*
I love you always,
Eloise

Alexander bowed his head and wept. Then, he left money
on the table to pay for the meal that never came and stumbled
back out to the car. In the evening, he stayed at a Super 8
motel, simply because of their advertised lobby computer. On
his arrest, the FBI had confiscated his cell phone, and of course
afterwards his computer, so that it was his first opportunity to
access the video mentioned by Robert Wilson.

After which, the terrible spectacle of Amy's mutilations –
the slashing of her face and grinding off of her fingers –
followed by her beheading left him sick and more shaken than
he'd ever been in his life. The video was sharply detailed,
leaving no doubt as to the competence of the producers. It was
titled "The Love Birds" (as the Imam had decreed), showing the
two – Amy and Benjamin - initially seated side by side as
"homecoming royalty" with gold paper crowns topped with
little crosses on their heads. Then, there followed a series of
dissolves to the various tortures, decapitation and crucifixion –
the violent scenes repeatedly rent with screams and howls from
Benjamin but strangely, Alexander thought, devoid of any
sound from Amy whatsoever. Grimly, he forced himself to
watch several times, focusing on Amy's face and detecting
several editorial "jump cuts" before in one fleeting sequence
able to see her lips move. He watched closely, again and again
– until he was sure that what she was saying was "Jesus is
Lord!" And he bowed his head again, overcome.

In their short time together, he'd had a true connection
with her – had loved her intelligence, her forthrightness and
fearlessness. And now his grieving escalated rapidly into a
raging fire for revenge, which nearly blinded him. He wanted to
kill them – *had to* kill them - but of course had no idea how to
get at them, or specifically who they were. The emotion was so

intense regarding her grisly killing, too, that the companion crucifixion of the unknown Benjamin seemed almost unimportant – save for his dangling of Amy's detached head by the hair on the way to his fate.

Alexander went to his room, but couldn't sleep. Then finally in the morning, decided he would head back home. He didn't know how he would fight, but knew that he *had to* fight. Telling himself that ultimately he'd be smart enough to adapt, and determined to find ways.

AFTERWORD

Vanishing!

High in the Wind River Range in Wyoming, looking down on the Wind River, in fact, a raggedly dressed man picked his way through rocks and scrub brush. He paused momentarily to examine a petroglyph etched in an outcropping by some member of the ancient tribe known as "The Sheepeaters," who'd migrated up from the Great Basin 3000 years earlier. "Lord Jesus!" the man breathed quietly, then continued on.

Further up the slope, he spotted a small flock of Big Horn Sheep, of the type that had drawn the Indians there; and he stood stock still, assessing the direction of the wind. Noting that it was coming from the animals and down the slope in his direction, he drew an arrow - or "rod" as they were sometimes called - from the quiver on his back; strung it in the powerful crossbow he'd been reduced to carrying; then started his deliberate, silent ascent.

Crouching often, staying behind boulders whenever possible, and with his heart pounding, not only from the exertion of the climb, he finally was within range. Lying on the ground, watching and selecting from several targets, choosing the largest, not for a trophy, but simply because it would feed him for the longest time.

He came to his feet, stumbling slightly but still able to let the arrow fly. Close enough to hear the "thunk" as it hit with shocking force and brought the sheep to its knees, and then over on the ground. And Jake Harwell knew that his existence could go on for at least a few more days.

THE END